Otherwise you can n' ...ought, had she come to such a
plea... ...ll grey stone houses with their moss-grown
...aute roofs seemed secretively withdrawn into some conspiracy against her.

Was that a face at a window? If so, the lace curtain flicked
down again before there was time for a full glimpse. Deborah,
town bred, was made uneasy by the silence . . .

Joan Aiken (1924–2004)

Joan Aiken, English-born daughter of American poet Conrad Aiken, began her writing career in the 1950s. Working for *Argosy* magazine as a copy editor but also as the anonymous author of articles and stories to fill up their pages, she was adept at inventing a wealth of characters and fantastic situations, and went on to produce hundreds of stories for *Good Housekeeping*, *Vogue*, *Vanity Fair* and many other magazines. Some of those early stories became novels, such as *The Silence of Herondale*, first published fifty years ago in 1964.

Although her first agent famously told her to stick to short stories, saying she would never be able to sustain a full-length novel, Joan Aiken went on to win the *Guardian* Children's Fiction Prize for *The Whispering Mountain*, and the Edgar Allan Poe award for her adult novel *Night Fall*. Her best known children's novel, *The Wolves of Willoughby Chase*, was acclaimed by *Time* magazine as 'a genuine small masterpiece'.

In 1999 she was awarded an MBE for her services to children's literature, and although best known as a children's writer, Joan Aiken wrote many adult novels, both modern and historical, with her trademark wit and verve. Many have a similar gothic flavour to her children's writing, and were much admired by readers and critics alike. As she said 'The only difference I can see is that children's books have happier endings than those for adults.' You have been warned . . .

By Joan Aiken
(Select bibliography of titles published in The Murder Room)

The Silence of Herondale (1964)
The Fortune Hunters (1965)
Trouble With Product X (1966)
Hate Begins at Home (1967)
The Ribs of Death (1967)
Died on a Rainy Sunday (1972)

The Silence of Herondale

Joan Aiken

An Orion Paperback

Copyright © Joan Aiken 1964

This edition published by
The Orion Publishing Group Ltd
Carmelite House
50 Victoria Embankment
London EC4Y 0DZ

An Hachette UK Company

10 9 8 7 6 5 4 3 2 1

A CIP catalogue record for this book is available from the British Library.

ISBN: 978 1 4719 2059 2

Printed and bound in Great Britain by Clays Ltd, Elcograf S.p.A.

MIX
Paper from
responsible sources
FSC www.fsc.org FSC® C104740

www.orionbooks.co.uk

Introduction to Joan Aiken's modern suspense novels

Best known for her children's books, such as *The Wolves of Willoughby Chase,* beloved by generations and still widely read today, Joan Aiken quickly established herself in the 1960s as a witty author of adult suspense with the ability to keep readers of all ages on the edge of their seats.

Too inventive to stick to a formula, she nevertheless revelled in the modern Gothic, and her novels were often compared with those of her contemporary, Mary Stewart. In the manner of Jane Austen's *Northanger Abbey*, Joan Aiken also gave her heroines a useful background in romantic fiction to support them through their frightful ordeals, as well as a quirky sense of humour, not unlike her own.

In true Gothic style these hapless heroines would become embroiled in a series of events not of their own making; while possessed of a certain charm – not just a literary education – their expectations did not lie in finding true love. They were, of course, always a version of Joan herself: small, red-haired, self-sufficient and fearless to the end. She sometimes made use of unlikely episodes from her own life, but learned an early lesson about using unvarnished experience: 'This is too improbable,' she was told by the editor of one story she had written flat from real life!

What she *could* guarantee were indefatigably sinister villains, finely controlled page-turning suspense, complex plots, and hair-raising climaxes, often with an unusually high body count . . .

As she confessed, 'I often have more characters than I know what to do with.'

Admired and enjoyed by many of her crime-writing contemporaries such as John Creasey, H.R.F. Keating, Francis Iles and Edmund Crispin, Joan Aiken's adult novels have lost none of their charm, and their now interestingly period settings – with endangered heroines who had to search for telephone boxes! – are sure to appeal to a new generation of readers who grew up on her wildly inventive children's books.

Lizza Aiken, 2019
Find more of Joan Aiken's modern novels on her website at http://www.joanaiken.com/

The hotel room was luxurious with the impersonal luxury of its kind: red roses and hothouse lilies stiffly arranged in corners to provide calculated splashes of colour; comfortable furniture—of the kind designed for superior waiting-rooms; tray of drinks and canapés on a coffee-table; the traffic noises of the Strand very muted and far away down below.

Deborah turned her eyes from the cheese-straws and swallowed, thrusting her hands deep into the pockets of her shabby coat. Her fingers folded and unfolded a ten-shilling note, the last money between her and her first week's salary.

If she was hired.

She brought her attention resolutely back to Marion Morne.

"You have no relatives at all?" Mrs Morne was saying. "Not even in Canada?"

"Not now. No." With all the energy she could summon, Deborah thrust away the memory of the little house under the maples as she had seen it last, before the sale, with her mother's sewing-machine covered, and gathering dust, the medical books in the study ranged into forlorn, neat heaps.

"What made you decide to come to England?"

Deborah said, thinking how callow the words sounded, "I want to be a writer. I heard there was more chance for writers over here—more chance to make a living, I mean."

1

She smiled a little wryly, thinking of the sheaf of rejection slips in her bedsitter.

"Have you given up the idea of writing, then?"

"Oh no. Or only temporarily." Deborah hesitated, wondering whether to mention the burglary; then she thought, no; her pride rebelled against letting this woman know how badly she needed the job.

"You have a degree . . . you were teaching in Canada . . ."

Deborah nodded, but she had the impression that Mrs Morne, turning over the application form in her long, jewelled fingers, was paying only token attention to her answers; the older woman's tone was vague as if some more remote problem occupied her mind. Were these not, Deborah began to wonder, rather unusually long-drawn-out preliminaries to consideration for what, surely, was an ordinary enough job of its kind? She had answered an advertisement in the *Times* personal column, had received a mimeographed form to complete with, so far as Deborah was concerned, mockingly and needlessly large spaces for qualifications, training, hobbies, "contacts"—why contacts?—and next of kin. In spite of the series of blanks in many of the spaces on her form, Deborah had then been summoned, among what seemed like a dauntingly large batch of other applicants, to a perfunctory interview in a small shabby office by a bored girl who merely checked through her completed form and interrogated her on it. More and more mystified, and beginning to be irritated, Deborah reiterated her list of negatives—no similar experience, no previous jobs in England, no, no family, no sponsors, no acquaintance in the theatrical world. And what in the name of goodness had *that* to do with the job in hand? If she had not by this time been so dispirited and cross, Deborah might have chuckled at the similarity between this screening for what had been advertised as a "pleasantly unusual opportunity for a gifted teacher with the right personality" and the sinister web that in the good old days lured innocent young girls off to a fate worse than death in Buenos Aires.

"Ridiculous set-up," sniffed a dignified, imposing woman —she could easily have been a headmistress—who had stood just ahead of Deborah in the line on the draughty stairs, and whom she had afterwards encountered again in the coffee-bar across the road. "From the fuss they're making you'd think the vacancy was for the principal of a college instead of a private tutorial job."

"Perhaps it's *King and I* stuff," suggested Deborah, her spirits raised by the extravagance of a cup of coffee. She knew she should not have succumbed to this temptation but the day was wet and the prospect gloomy; if academic qualifications were what counted, all the other applicants looked as if they had more; this woman probably had the lot, from B.A. to Ph. Zool.

"King and I?" The woman stared at her uncomprehendingly.

"You know—tutoring the child of an oriental potentate."

"They all go to Eton now," her neighbour said with finality.

"Okay—then the job's for Education Minister in one of the new African countries."

"I think that's *most* unlikely."

Thoroughly snubbed, Deborah sighed, and remarked, "Well I daresay we shall never know," picked up her purse, and left to start on the long, wet walk back to her lodgings, resolving to dismiss the whole affair from her mind and try for something else. She had been astonished, three days later, to be summoned for what was apparently a short-list interview with Mrs Morne, who, she learned, was guardian to the prospective pupil. Were other applicants also being seen? There had been no sign of any. Yet Mrs Morne's manner was so vague and distant that Deborah would not allow herself to hope that she was the only candidate who had made the grade. Such an idea seemed preposterous.

Mrs Morne's manner might be vague, but her eyes were shrewd, assessing Deborah's threadbare coat and gloves, the two-years-out-of-fashion Canadian shoes and weather-beaten purse, as shabby as it was empty. Mrs Morne's smoke-grey dress and furs were the sort seen more often in fashion magazines than in real life, and her fine oval face was witness to the beauty salon's art, but her dark eyes were lined and wary. Her mouth, her posture, the very

3

movements of her hands spoke of a self-discipline that by
now had become second nature.

"It was brave to come over here all alone," Mrs Morne
said with a warmth which, like everything else about her,
seemed carefully measured.

"Oh well—" Deborah smiled uncomfortably, thinking,
I wish she'd hurry up and say whether I've got the job or
not. I suppose they'll be letting me know in a day or two.
I'll buy a loaf and some cheese on the way home—there's
still a spoonful of coffee left. I suppose I'll have to move to
a hostel for down-and-outs when the rent falls due on
Saturday . . . Mrs Morne was still looking at her, so she
added, "There was nothing to keep me in Canada, really."

"Both your parents are dead?"

All the information was there on the form before her,
but Deborah patiently repeated yet again that her father,
a country doctor in New Brunswick, had been killed last
winter, with his wife, when another car skidded and ran
into them as they drove home along icy roads from a medical convention in Montreal.

"You were fond of your parents?" Mrs Morne said
suddenly.

"Yes—very." Deborah tried to banish the gruffness from
her voice. The question was harmless, natural enough, yet
it hardly seemed in keeping with the impression she had
formed of Mrs Morne. But the woman really seemed interested, as if she wanted to know. Why? Evidence as to
character?

"Tell me about your father. What was he like?"

"He was a happy man," Deborah said slowly. "His life
was quite simple. He knew what needed doing and he did
it. Every life he saved was another tally on his score—and
he saved a lot. He had that kind of directness in everything he did. My mother—" She checked a moment, then
ended, "I'm glad for her that she was with him in the car.
It was quick. I couldn't imagine them separated."

"But it came hard on you," Mrs Morne said quickly.
"You say you have no other relatives at all—I hope there
were friends to help you with all the wretched practical
arrangements—?"

4

"Oh, yes—yes, there were." Somehow, without being aware of how it came about, Deborah found herself launched on a rambling account of her childhood, which, in its unpretentious happiness and simplicity, mirrored the characters of her two parents. Both were of Scottish descent, both had the profound Lowland respect for book-learning and straight dealing; everybody in the little town where they lived had held them in trust and affection. Doctor Lindsay and "Mrs Doc" were inevitably the arbiters in any problem or trouble; at their unpretentious funeral the entire town had turned out and the wreaths were piled deep. The Doctor had died a poor man, however, due to his habit of giving liberally to any deserving cause, especially cancer research, and letting his patients' bills run high; Deborah had had to sell the little house under the maples to pay the debts. Several neighbours would have been glad to help her finish her college career but she had an independent nature which was mistaken by some for standoffishness; she preferred to manage on her own, tutoring and baby-sitting. This, coupled with the fact that she seldom went back to her home-town—really, she could hardly bear to, and what was there to draw her now the little house was occupied by strangers?—had militated against her. Her motives were misunderstood, she was saddled with the stigma of being snobbish, citified, "thinking herself better than her folks." Working desperately hard at her degree course to drown sad memories, Deborah was hardly aware of loneliness until she had graduated and taken a job teaching school for a year. But by then, in any case, she had met Patrick . . .

"No relatives at all," Mrs Morne said musingly. "It's quite an unusual state, really. But I can sympathise. Most of my family are dead: two out of my three brothers. And the eldest, John, is very ill now, up in Yorkshire . . ."

"I'm so sorry." But as Deborah spoke the conventional phrase she thought that this woman gave no sign of bereavement or anxiety; it was hard to imagine her as a little girl with her brothers, eagerly carrying their fishing-tackle, fielding for them, begging to be allowed to accompany them on excursions. She did not, somehow, suggest family ties.

"Is he—the brother who's ill—the little girl's father?" Deborah asked. She had gathered that the prospective pupil was a girl, but nothing more.

"Who—? Oh, Carreen. No, her parents died in an air-crash five years ago when she was eight. I've looked after her since then. My brother in Yorkshire never married—he lives like a hermit—and the middle brother, Laurence, was drowned in a yachting accident."

"I see," said Deborah, struggling to keep a clear picture of this genealogical tangle—but anyway, surely she need hardly concern herself with three brothers, two of whom were dead and one gravely ill in Yorkshire. "And he—the middle brother—had no children?"

"His wife left him. I understand there was a boy but his mother took him with her—we've lost touch years ago. She's in America I believe . . . She never made any offer to help with Carreen, at all events."

"Carreen is thirteen?"

"Yes . . . Well," said Mrs Morne, suddenly coming briskly to the point as if, during this rather aimless family talk, she had been summing up Deborah and had now reached her decision, "as you realise, Carreen is a very special child. She has lived with me in the south of France since her parents died—"

"She's been going to a French school?" Deborah asked.

"School? No—good heavens, no schools." Mrs Morne's tone dismissed the whole scholastic system with scorn. "She would hardly benefit from school—or have time for it. No, I have taught her—what was necessary. But now we may be obliged to live in England for some months on—on account of my elder brother's state of health. I may have to drop all my own activities and deal with his business affairs, so I shall have less time for Carreen. And English regulations about children's education are so pettifogging . . ."

Mrs Morne had a trick of letting her voice trail off at the end of a remark which left Deborah curiously ill at ease.

"Carreen's been ill," Mrs Morne went on irritably. "Measles with complications. Our doctor said sea air—so we've been cruising. But she's still rather moody and listless. However," her mouth closed with a sudden snap, "it's high time she got back to work."

Deborah's heart sank at the picture of Carreen she was assembling from Mrs Morne's remarks—a delicate, illiterate, probably spoilt brat, used to a life among adults on the Riviera.

"She and Willie are flying in this evening."

Mrs Morne, Deborah had vaguely gathered, was a widow, so who was Willie? To her polite look of inquiry Mrs Morne explained, "Willie's our Press Agent. He's arranged for a press conference at five."

"A *press* conference?" By now Deborah was right out of her depth. She could see that Mrs Morne was a wealthy woman, but surely she was not a celebrity on this scale?

"Well, of course, everyone's dying to know if Carreen's finished another play. Unfortunately the answer is that she hasn't, on account of the illness and convalescence."

"A play?" Deborah was suddenly illuminated. "Good heavens, do you mean that your niece is *Carreen Gilmartin?*"

"Yes, hadn't you realised? Oh, how stupid of me." Mrs Morne smiled perfunctorily, but her eyes remained aloof and scrutinising. Deborah felt snubbed, and suddenly decided that she disliked this woman with her languid mannerisms and her curiously flat voice from which all trace of character had been ironed out, leaving a well-bred blankness.

"But in that case—" Deborah pushed herself with decision out of the awkwardly low-slung chair—"you'll surely be wanting someone with far more qualifications than mine to look after her? If I'd known I'd never have wasted your time by applying—"

"Oh, not at all, my dear." To her surprise, Mrs Morne quickly crossed the room and gave her two little pats on the shoulder, like an accolade. Her smile now had real warmth and her voice was amused and friendly. "It's someone just like you that I've been hoping for—young, natural, not too impressed by Carreen's reputation. I deliberately kept her name out of the advertisement because I didn't want to be deluged with applications from stage-struck females and people who thought it would be a way into show business. But I can see that you're not a bit like that. I'm delighted with you, Miss—"

"Lindsay."

"Lindsay, of course. I think you're just the person I want. You're intelligent, with teaching experience, but not hidebound, you write a bit yourself, you've no ties—you wouldn't object to travelling?"

"Heavens, no!"

"That's excellent. In general we lead quite a nomadic life. Are you engaged? Any fiancé in the background?"

"No," Deborah said clearly, and shut her heart against the little cold pang that recalled Patrick in Toronto. Six hours' time difference: Patrick enjoying a gay breakfast with his two months' bride, waving her goodbye as she set off for rehearsal.

"The job's yours." Mrs Morne's tone was flat, incisive; Debhorah fought and quelled the impulse to say, "I've decided I don't want it," as Mrs Morne mentioned a generous salary. Instead she asked,

"When would you like me to start?"

"Now," said Mrs Morne, smiling again. "The job—as you've gathered—will be much more than just teaching. I want you to be companion, help, friend, and general adviser. Right now Carreen's going to need some new clothes, she has nothing suitable for late November in England. Here are her measurements on this card; I'd like you to go along to Port and Bellingham's, I've an account there, and get her this list of things. The warm topcoat is important—she'll want that at once—and so is the dress. I'd like something she can wear at the press conference. Not too adult. All her French clothes are too sophisticated; I want the reporters to see her as the little girl she really is. Get something *young*—blue velveteen, perhaps, with a white collar or smocking—something like that. You see?"

"Wouldn't it be better to wait till she arrives?" Deborah said dubiously.

Mrs Morne looked slightly impatient. "There's no time now," she said. "You can go shopping with her again later on. Oh, and get her a skirt and sweater and windcheater in case we have to go to Yorkshire suddenly. The latest news of my brother is not at all good."

Her eyes flicked momentarily to a small desk where letters lay scattered.

"And of course get her gloves, hood, scarf, warm underwear, stockings—oh, and some hair-ribbons. Charge it all to my account."

"What colouring is she?" Deborah asked.

"Colouring?" Mrs Morne looked vague.

"Dark or fair?"

"Oh, dark. Dark, takes after her father." Mrs Morne's mouth thinned. "Yes, she's a dark little thing. Like yourself . . . Now, let me see. When you've done that, come straight back here. She and Willie should arrive at about half past four and the press conference starts as soon as Carreen's tidied up."

Poor child, thought Deborah, what an ordeal: stepping straight off a plane to face a press conference in a new dress bought for you at random by a stranger. But I suppose she's used to such experiences; Mrs Morne certainly seems to have her life thoroughly in hand.

Mrs Morne was undoubtedly an expert at the management of people in an unobtrusive fashion: Deborah found herself neatly organised out of the room and into the hotel lift, still clutching the list of articles to be bought, and Carreen's measurements, in her hand.

So! she thought, shivering in the Strand as the raw November wind sliced through her worn tweed, I'm to teach sums and spelling to Carreen Gilmartin. What an extraordinary job to have landed. Patrick would be amused . . .

She had met Patrick at the very end of her final year in college. Someone taking a walk-on part in the college play—*Flora MacDonald*—had broken a leg, and Deborah, who had the right appearance, had been called upon to stand in at the last minute. The costume had suited her. And so had the carefree light-heartedness of the group who formed the rest of the cast. Relaxing after the tension of her final examinations—and by dogged hard work she had done well; her father would have been proud of her—she allowed herself to fall a little bit in love with the whole group. They were the family she lacked. Patrick, a rising young producer, was in charge, and, as well, taking the part of Charles Edward. In him the group's intelligence and charm were epitomised—and while Deborah was mistaking intelligence in him for sympathy, he was powerfully attracted by her candour, by her looks, by the straightforwardness in her grey eyes contrasted against the veiled but cut-throat competition among the young Method actresses he usually went round with.

By the end of a week they were engaged, and all Patrick's ex-girl friends were prophesying doom. "She's just a dumb cluck, he'll be bored with it in a month," was the general view. But Deborah was not dumb and it was precisely this, and her passion for analysis, for seeing things clearly, which led to the ultimate break-up six months later. She longed to know all about Patrick. With her parents' fondness for thoroughly investigating the motives and morals of a situation—oh, those long, easy, comfortable, soul-baring discussions over the dishes, or the weeding, or the corn-hulling!—Deborah most innocently wanted to learn all she could about what made Patrick tick. It never occurred to her that a fitfully brilliant, moody, charming young man might not want to be known in this way.

Scared to death by what he had landed himself in, Patrick did not consciously set out to be unkind. Like a wild thing caught in a trap he merely struggled frantically to extricate himself, lashing about somewhat in the process, and seized the first plausible means of escape that presented itself: a young Toronto actress with influential friends in TV. Deborah, after some desperate months and a few small literary successes which she hardly noticed in her wretchedness, decided to cut her losses and go to England. She had nothing to lose. Now, a year later, she was able to realise that she had been lucky to escape with some mental bruises and badly shaken confidence; marriage to Patrick would have been a disaster for both of them. She spared a wry grin, now, for talented Patrick—he wrote plays, too—and wondered what his comment would be on the job she had landed. But then, of course, Patrick had little interest in any position save his own, and doubtless he had the lowest possible opinion of little Careen Gilmartin's precocious gift.

A theatre poster on a hoarding caught Deborah's eye. Torn and old, it flapped in the bitter wind:

Diadem Theatre
TO CROWN THE UNICORN
ew play by
rreen Gilmartin

What would it be like trying to teach history and geography to someone who apparently had, at the age of thirteen, more insight into the geography of the human heart than most people acquired in the whole of their lives? Four plays by Carreen Gilmartin had been produced on the London stage; one was filmed already, another filming.

To Deborah it seemed an impertinence that she, who had done nothing more unusual than live quietly in Canada all her twenty years, let herself be jilted by a handsome young opportunist, have a few articles accepted, and sail to the Old World, should presume to teach this prodigy. It seemed absurd to be buying dresses and hair-ribbons for her as if she were an ordinary child.

Impulsively, Deborah spent half a crown out of the ten shillings—when would Mrs Morne pay her first instalment of salary, she wondered—on a paperback edition of *To Crown the Unicorn,* and slipped it into the deep pocket of her coat. She would read it over supper. There would still be enough money for the loaf and cheese . . .

Port and Bellingham's, in the full preen of Christmas display, offered a mocking, glittering criss-cross of aisles festooned with coloured lights, counters piled high with gloves, jewellery, and sheer stockings, shelves of perfumes and handbags, racks of elegant warm coats, mouth-watering displays of candies and crystallised fruits—to someone with seven-and-six in her pocket. Deborah eyed the counters dispassionately and mounted with the escalator to the girls' wear department.

She bought a camel-hair coat—and then paused, baffled at the problem of choosing a dress for a child she had never seen. Pulling the paperback from her pocket she studied the photograph on the cover. In the manner of its kind it showed a face that might have been any age from ten to thirty-five—a serious, wide-eyed face with dark, straight, shoulder-length hair.

Deborah decided that Carreen didn't look like a child who would be fussy about her clothes. She bought a scarlet wind-cheater and navy-blue pleated skirt, and what she hoped Mrs Morne would consider a suitable dress for the press conference, grey velveteen with a white collar.

Underwear, stockings. What now? She consulted the list again. Gloves, hair-ribbons. Downstairs again to the haberdashery which lay beyond umbrellas and watches and jewellery.

The warmth, and the incessant jostling of fretful Christmas shoppers began to make Deborah feel very tired. She realised again how hungry she was. Pushing away the thought of food, she wished instead that she had enough money to buy a present for Carreen. She paused, considering a necklace of green carved beads linked to a fine, airy silver chain, before she remembered that its price was quite beyond her reach. She moved on, laughing at herself ruefully in the counter mirror, as she did so catching the eye of the thin, fair salesgirl, who looked tired to death.

"Miss Simmons!" snapped a man's voice beside Deborah. The fair girl jumped guiltily. "I can see a customer who's been waiting several minutes!"

The girl hurried down the counter to where a stout young man was gesturing towards a lavish rhinestone necklace. The man who had galvanised her, a sharp, foxy-faced character beside Deborah, moved on, casting a practised eye this way and that over the jostling aisles and the harrassed assistants.

Deborah bought scarlet gloves and hood, a rainbow

handful of red, blue, pink, and yellow ribbons. Slowly she fought her way through the crowd to the street entrance, glancing at her watch. Carreen's press conference was at five—she would be in good time. Outside in the street the light was turning a nebulous blue; wet pavements reflected colours from Christmas-lit windows and a delicate drizzle crinkled the paper of the parcels Deborah carried.

She could not help a faint prick of excitement at this rather heart-warmingly festive task of carrying parcels home to a little girl, and found herself hoping that Carreen would like the grey dress, that the hair-ribbons would go with the child's eyes—what colour had Mrs Morne said they were—blue?

It was only five minutes' walk from Port and Bellingham's to the Arundel Hotel—not worth clawing on and off a bus, laden as she was. She walked it, thinking cheerfully that at least luck had been on her side in that she had been wearing her really waterproof shoes the day her room had been burgled. She had been out studying the newspaper ad. columns in the local public library, since English editors had not proved encouraging and her savings were running alarmingly low. She had returned to find clothes, books, money, her few trinkets, and, most crushing blow of all, her typewriter, all missing. It had seemed to her astonishing that someone thought it worth stealing such a poverty-stricken little handful of belongings, but apparently someone had. And of course none of it was insured and the police held out no hope of recovering anything; as her landlady told her, she might think herself lucky the thieves had done no structural damage, or she might have been held responsible for that too.

Oh well, Deborah thought, pausing to survey the pink-lit glass-panelled foyer of the Arundel Hotel appreciatively, maybe my luck's turned now. If only Carreen is a likeable child. But the salary's almost suspiciously good. She's sure to be a little horror.

She glanced at the rack of evening papers to see if there were headlines about the wonder child playwright flying in —but they were heavily concerned with the escape of a homicidal maniac from Broadmoor—and scanned the foyer for possible signs of Carreen's arrival. There were none. Two men, and a girl with a vaguely familiar face came through the swing doors as she pressed the lift button, and paused to consult the receptionist. Deborah let the doors close and the lift carry her upwards with her load of damp parcels. Who could the girl be? One of the other applicants for the job that she had seen at the dingy office?

"Carreen's clothes? Good," said Mrs Morne absently. "Now, be an angel and just check through this list of invitations with me, will you—oh, put the things in Carreen's room first, could you, the next in the suite through mine— that door there; thanks."

Deborah came back reflecting that being guardian to a prodigy-playwright must be a paying profession, unless Mrs Morne also had a handsome private income. A knock sounded on the door as she picked up the list of names and a pencil.

"Come in!" called Mrs Morne.

Two men and a girl entered—the trio Deborah had noticed downstairs. Now the girl's face came back to her—it was the fair-haired assistant from the costume-jewellery counter at Port and Bellingham's.

"Excuse me, madam, I wonder if we might trouble you for a few minutes?"

That was the foxy man who had admonished the girl. And the third was a fleshy, pinstriped individual with the pasted-on solemnity of a hired mute at a funeral.

"What is it?" said Mrs Morne irritably. "I'm very busy just now."

"We're from Port and Bellingham's, madam. It's about the young lady here."

The foxy man gestured at Deborah who had a sudden uncomfortable feeling of hollowness at the stomach and dryness at the mouth—she could not for the life of her imagine why.

"What about her?" Mrs Morne looked at her watch impatiently. "You mean because she bought those clothes and charged them to my account? That's perfectly in order, she bought them for me. And you know *me*, I should hope."

"Oh yes, Mrs Morne, of course we do. Of course," he said, smiling so as to show every tooth in a handsome set. "No, it was about the necklace. We wondered if that was to be charged to your account too, madam, as the young lady never mentioned it."

"Necklace? What necklace? What is all this about?" Mrs Morne snapped, looking from the foxy man to Deborah.

"I don't know. There must be some mistake, surely?" Deborah said, doing her best to fight down unreasoning nervousness.

"What necklace?" Mrs Morne asked the man again. "Do hurry up, I've only five minutes."

"Why, the necklace the young lady took without paying for."

"I didn't take a necklace!" Deborah exclaimed in astonished indignation. "You must be mistaking me for someone else!"

"Oh, but you did, miss. A silver chain with imitation jade stones. Both I and Miss Simmons here distinctly saw you take it."

"What utter *nonsense*—" Deborah began, and simultaneously Mrs Morne said, "This is ridiculous. You must be confusing her with another person."

"Oh, no, madam. That is the young lady, isn't it, Miss Simmons?"

Plainly terrified, Miss Simmons whispered, "Yes, that's her. She put it in her pocket."

"Perhaps you wouldn't mind turning your pockets out, miss?"

"I do rather object," said Deborah with spirit, plunging her hands into the pockets of her shabby coat, "but if it will get this—" Her voice faded away and she stood and stared with a slowly whitening face at the collection of objects she had pulled out—a handkerchief, the paperback edition of Carreen's play, a selection of bus tickets, and the green necklace that she had considered buying for a present.

"That's the one!" the foxy man said triumphantly. "Imitation jade, twenty-five and six. The ticket's still on it with our code."

He pointed to the little square of pasteboard dangling on its string.

"But this is stupid. It must be a mistake!" protested Deborah. "I didn't take it, I wouldn't think of doing such a thing! I'm not—" Not that sort of person, she had been going to say, but she stopped. After all, what did these people know about her? With a chill of dismay she began to realise how you shed your identity in a strange country where you have no one to vouch for you. "It must somehow have been knocked off into my pocket," she ended lamely. "Please believe me—and for goodness' sake take it back! I honestly didn't steal it."

"They all say that," she heard the fleshy man murmur to the girl.

"Look," Deborah said, trying to speak calmly. "I do absolutely promise you that this was an accident. It must have caught on my cuff strap or something—I was looking at it, certainly, thinking I'd like to buy it for a present—I thought it would be nice to give to Carreen," she said with a faint smile to Mrs Morne, who returned the look blankly —"and then I realised I hadn't enough money so I put it back. *I didn't take it!* I don't *do* things like that! Nothing like this has ever happened to me before, I—"

"Obviously the whole thing is an unfortunate mistake," Mrs Morne said, her high weary voice cutting through Deborah's appeal. "Miss Lindsay, who is in my employment, assures you that she didn't take the necklace, so let that be the end of the matter."

"But—" the foxy man began. She ignored him.

"As it's here I'll buy the necklace—my niece will like it—and that will settle the whole business nicely, won't it?" She smiled a wholly artificial smile at the four of them, and her dark eyes came to rest reflectively on Deborah.

"That's not really satisfactory, madam," the fleshy man began.

"Why not?" Mrs Morne said coldly. "If I vouch for Miss Lindsay you should be satisfied."

"Has she been in your employment long, madam?"

Deborah felt her face redden and cursed herself. Why

was it so appallingly easy to feel guilty when one was perfectly innocent?

"No," said Mrs Morne, "but I am perfectly satisfied with her references."

It sounds like a kitchen-maid, Deborah thought.

"You see, madam, we've got to protect ourselves and our other customers. Normally with a first shoplifting offence—"

"I am *not* a shoplifter!" Deborah burst out.

"—As I was saying, normally we take a photo of the person's face and stick it up on our staff notice-board. It is the duty of the staff to memorise these faces, and then if such an occurrence were to 'appen—happen again they would be forewarned. So if you don't mind, madam, I'll just do this—"

Without more ado he pulled a small camera from his pocket and snapped Deborah, whose mouth opened in angry protest just too late.

"Very well, then, madam, if you're satisfied with the young lady's story, we'll call ourselves satisfied too, now," he said, pocketing the camera again. "And we'll charge the necklace to your account. Miss Simmons, just make out an invoice, will you?"

"And hurry up, *please*," Mrs Morne snapped. "This whole business has been a ridiculous and deplorable waste of my time."

The fair girl quickly and nervously scribbled a formula on a pad, the foxy man gave the necklace to Mrs Morne, who dropped it irritably into an ashtray, and the three took their departure.

Deborah felt sick and bruised. With an effort she faced Mrs Morne, who had reseated herself and gone containedly back to her list of invitees as if nothing out of the ordinary had happened.

"That was very—very kind of you," Deborah said, and was surprised to find her voice so level.

The dark reflective eyes met hers.

"It was nothing," Mrs Morne said gently. "People like that are easily dealt with."

"Still, I'm extremely grateful. You're sure that—that in

the circumstances you don't want to reconsider my application—You do really believe my story?"

"Of *course* I do, my dear. Of *course* I do." Mrs Morne's smile was as sweet and slow as her words. "Well, that's that. Let's think no more of the matter, shall we? But . . ." She looked at Deborah straight and unblinkingly. Was there a threat behind her stare? "Let's have no repetitions of this kind of fuss, Miss Lindsay, shall we? I've got you out of this little predicament, but I can't keep doing that kind of thing. We don't want any *more* photographs of you put up on staff notice-boards."

A taxi drew up outside the Arundel Hotel and two people got out. While the man was paying off the driver the small girl who was with him slipped ahead into the foyer and put a question to the plump, fatherly commissionaire. He nodded, and took her to the reception desk, where the clerk handed her a letter. Her eyes lit up; she opened it and rapidly read the half-dozen lines it contained.

"Can you tell me how to get to this address?" she asked the receptionist.

"Yes, miss. You'd have to take a train."

"Is it quite a long way?"

"Fair distance. I'll look it up for you in a moment—just excuse me while I answer my phone—"

"Never mind just now, thank you. I'll came back later perhaps," the child said quickly, slipping the letter into her pocket. At that moment her companion came through the swing doors and glanced round to see where she was.

"Carrie? Ah, there you are. Quick, my dear, we must spruce ourselves for your admirers—there will be time for a bath if you hurry—"

He took her arm and bustled her into the lift. The doors slid to behind them.

Deborah opened her mouth to speak, to say to Mrs Morne, You can keep your job, I've decided I'd sooner work in an undertaker's parlour laying out corpses than have anything more to do with you, but at that moment the door opened, briskly, abruptly. A short slight man walked into the room, said, without preamble, "Marion, the newspapermen are beginning to arrive. Should you not be downstairs keeping an eye on them?"

"Willie! When did you get here?"

"Oh, five minutes ago. I have been checking in. The child is in her room. Everything is running smoothly?"

"Yes, yes," Mrs Morne said impatiently. She ruffled herself into her furs, picked up a crocodile-and-gold bag, glanced unflusteredly round the room, and said, "You'll bring the child down, will you? Oh—this is Miss Lindsay, who's going to be teaching Carreen from now on," smiled another of her sweet, flicked-on smiles, and was gone.

This is a mad situation and I'm not staying in it, Deborah decided. I don't have to and I won't. I don't owe Mrs Morne a thing. It would be impossible to work for someone who believes I'm a shoplifter.

"You'll help Carrie tidy herself up, will you, Miss Lindsay?" the man called Willie said in a friendly voice.

In spite of her mentally beaten-up state Deborah could not restrain a faint prick of curiosity at the thought of the child playwright.

I'll help her dress and tidy, and then I'll go, she resolved. She looked up, found Willie's inquisitive pale eyes studying her, and nodded.

"She's having a quick bath but she'll be out directly," he went on. "So Marion's picked you for our good fairy, has she?" His English was rapid and fluent, but heavily accented in a thick, middle-European manner.

He was a very foreign-looking man altogether, Deborah thought: nearly bald, and his mobile face, with its pointed, slightly twisted nose was an odd greyish colour. The whites of his eyes were yellow and liverish. He wore a square-cut grey alpaca suit, immensely thick-soled shoes, and a white carnation in his buttonhole. Deborah smiled in acknowledgment of his little bow and he said quickly, "I introduce myself. I am Willie Rienz, Carreen's public relations officer, as you have probably gathered.—I think it is now time you encouraged her to come out of her bath."

"Of course," Deborah said, and went through Mrs Morne's bedroom. A few childish possessions were scattered in the smaller room beyond—three or four little ornamental glass animals, a pair of size two velvet slippers, a Swiss silk dress, evidently just discarded, a couple of books; but of the owner there was no sign. Some of the parcels left by Deborah had been opened; the wrappings lay strewn on the bed.

"Carreen?" Deborah called hesitatingly. "Are you in the bath?"

No one answered. But her eye was caught next moment by a sheet of paper lying in the centre of the dressing-table. It had a message written on it in large round letters.

The message said:

> *I cannot write any more plays for you and I do not wish to talk about it at the moment. I have a chance to go away so I am going, but I will get in touch with you later. Please do not inform the police or worry about me. I am grateful for all you have done, but it is essential that I should have freedom of mind.*
>
> CARREEN.

Willie's voice called, "Where is the little tyke?" He came into the room.

Deborah was still staring at the message.

"She has not gone off shopping or something disastrous like that, has she?" he said.

"I don't know," Deborah said doubtfully. "I found this. What do you suppose it means?" She handed him the note.

As he read it, Deborah had the impression that a frighteningly cold gleam of rage came into his narrowed eyes, but the next moment he looked up at her and she decided that she must have imagined it.

"What a little cuss!" he said laughing. "Just wait till Marion sees this. Then the fur will fly! We had better find the naughty child quickly."

"Where can she be?"

"You put your finger on the problem." He reflected. "We have not been in England since her parents were alive; they had a house in Oxford. She might have gone to friends there. Maybe. Or there is a place in Devonshire where they spent a holiday on a farm—she used to talk about it a great deal. Another possibility. Or she might have made for Yorkshire—to Marion's eldest brother, John—she has also stayed with him when her parents were alive. On the whole I think that is the most likely. I think she has not been told he was ill."

"That gives a good deal of scope, though, doesn't it," Deborah said dubiously. "Shall you tell the police?"

"Dear me, no. That would be most unfortunate publicity. Marion would not like it at all. She will be so angry! I am sorry for the child if she is not found and made to see reason pretty soon. Marion can be—formidable."

"But surely Carreen is—well, old enough to make decisions for herself? You can't expect her to be treated like an ordinary child?"

But his last statement went on ringing in her ears, and she felt a chill of apprehension on behalf of the unknown Carreen at the thought of Mrs Morne's reaction to this escapade.

"You don't think it could be a case of kidnapping?" she suggested.

"I doubt it. It would be better for Carrie, in a way, if it was. And *that* would be excellent publicity. But—no. We ought to have seen this coming. Since her illness, Carrie has been unusually quiet and withdrawn. She has grown a lot in the last few months—mentally and physically."

"What is she like?" Deborah asked impulsively.

"A nice little child. Intelligent. But it is not intelligent to run away from Marion. Carreen is no match for Marion, and she is Marion's bread-and-butter—unless John dies."

"The brother in Yorkshire?"

"Yes. He, you understand, is an immensely wealthy man —factories, house property, land—so forth. All the heart can desire. And Marion is his only sister. And he is very ill. But he may recover.—No, you see it is essential Carrie should be found quickly." He gave Deborah a swift, measuring look. "You know, I think it highly probable that she has gone to Yorkshire to see her uncle; I am wondering if you had not better take a train and go up there too."

"I'm afraid I'm not staying in this job. I've decided I

don't want to work for Mrs Morne," Deborah said lightly and firmly.

"Oh, what nonsense, my dear. You do not wish to leave that poor little child to face Marion's wrath all on her own, do you?" he said smiling. "Besides—no, I shouldn't come to that decision if I were you. Marion is a very good, generous employer, I promise you—*so long* as you give satisfaction. But she would think it most disloyal if you were to leave now, in this emergency. I strongly advise you to pack a nightdress, like a good girl, and catch a train up to Yorkshire."

"But—it's absurd. Why can't you just ring up Mr—Mr Gilmartin?"

"You forget—old John is very ill—he may even be in hospital. There is a housekeeper, Mrs Thingummy—Lewthwaite—but she is rather deaf, and rapidly becomes flustered on the telephone; ring her up with a story about a missing little girl and she will probably fly into a panic and give the old man a dose of disinfectant instead of medicine. And, in any case, what will be the use? *She* cannot persuade Carrie to come home. Besides, even if Carrie is on her way, she will not arrive for some hours yet."

"But her uncle could send her back?"

"He is too ill, my dear. Besides," said Willie delicately, "he is not on *very* good terms with Marion. Particularly if Carreen comes to him with some tale of woe. It is even doubtful if he would feel inclined to help. It would really be better if Carreen did not see and upset him."

This rang oddly to Deborah and hardly accorded with the probable legacy—or Mrs Morne's explanation of her long stay in England to help with her brother's affairs— but still, Deborah reminded herself, it was none of her business.

"So, you just run along to Herondale," Willie pursued, sounding as if Yorkshire were just a mile or two north of Regent's Park, "and if Carrie is there, talk some sense into her, persuade her not to bother her uncle, and bring her back. Marion will be so pleased with you and it will all be for the best. Meanwhile I will be telephoning the friends in Oxford and Devon."

"Where is this place?" Deborah said.

He snapped his fingers. "What is the address again? Ah, I know—" They had moved back into Mrs Morne's sitting-room and he searched on the desk until he found the letter he wanted. "Here we have it—Herondale House, Herondale, Cranton, Yorkshire." He tore off the strip of letter-heading and gave it to her. "They will tell you downstairs in Reception how to get there. You go to Leeds, I think, and then change. There is indubitably a night train and it will be best for you to get it."

Deborah glanced at the slip of paper. *Yorkshire*, and below it, in a sprawling, uneducated handwriting, the words *Dear Mrs Mor*— Where was Yorkshire? Quite a long way off, surely?

"I haven't any money," she said, stalling.

Willie Rienz peeled notes off a thick wad and gave them to her. "There you are. Now, do not delay. At this very moment you may be missing a train, who knows? Carreen may even be on it. I will tell Marion what happened—she will be pleased with you—and inform the press that Carrie is sick. You will telephone when you reach Herondale, will you not?"

"Oh, very well," said Deborah, but still hesitated, feeling —she could not tell why—oddly uneasy. "But what can I— why should *I* have any effect? And shouldn't I see Mrs Morne myself?"

He was impatient. "Not necessary! She is busy charming the press-men. And they are going to need plenty of charming. I will tell Marion later, you may be sure she will approve your expedition. And—Miss Lindsay—if Carreen is there you *must* persuade her to come back! This is most important! If you had ever seen Marion in one of her rages —you would want to help that poor little child! And Marion's anger when she is roused is apt to be *widespread*—"

His fingers pressed hard—significantly?—into Deborah's shoulder and he urged her towards the door. "And of course, Miss Lindsay, I need not remind you—the utmost discretion please! This is not a story for the public." He was smiling, but there was an unmistakable warning in his eyes. With a firm hand he shut the door behind her.

Beyond the pink-lit foyer a bitter wind with a hint of sleet in it was scouring the empty Strand. Road and pavements shone like black ice.

Having learned from the Arundel reception desk that one reached Yorkshire by rail via St Pancras station, Deborah extravagantly took a taxi to her lodgings in Marchmont Street, where she packed the remaining handful of her rifled belongings into a bag.

She then went down to the basement and found her landlady in her sluttish kitchen as usual, dispiritedly filling in breakfast-food competition forms over a cup of cold tea.

"'Why I would like to own a Dream House' in twenty words," she said. "What shall I put? 'I 'ave always wanted a breakfast nook and laundry area like the one in your picture, besides no stairs and a walk-in airing cupboard and larder—'"

"Too long," Deborah said. "Why don't you just put 'So I can kick out all my lodgers and live a life of my own'?"

"Ah, that's it, love, that's just the ticket. There, you see wot it is bein' able to write, you can put it in a nutshell. I bet you 'it the jackpot one of these days, see your name in lights. 'Ave you 'ad any stories accepted yet?"

"Not yet," Deborah said. "So I've taken a job to tide me over. In fact I've come to give notice, Mrs Tidbury, and to say goodbye—I've got to go off to Yorkshire right away."

"Yorkshire? Well I never!" Mrs Tidbury laid down her ballpoint and gazed at Deborah in astonishment. "Goin' off today? What ever are you goin' to do up there?"

"Be a governess—teach a little girl. Quite a famous little girl, in fact—Carreen Gilmartin, the child who writes plays."

"Go-ood gracious me! Fancy that! Carreen Gilmartin, I saw her on telly once."

"What was she like?" Deborah asked curiously.

Mrs Tidbury primmed up her lips.

"Quiet. Clever. Not what I'd call a talking child. I expect it was mostly shyness, though," she added scrupulously. "The quiet ones are shy, aren't they? Still, she wasn't the sort I'd go for meself—I like a child to *act* more like a child —more like my sister's Julie. But I expect you'll get on with her all right, dear, bein' so clever yerself."

Since Deborah had seen the Julie in question several times and considered her an odious, frilled, ringleted, spoiled, niminy-piminy brat she reserved judgment on Mrs Tidbury's pronouncement, and said instead,

"I've cleared and packed my things, Mrs T., what's left of them, and my room's tidy, and I've folded the sheets. I'll be saying goodbye, then and thanks for having me—"

"Eh, well, I hate to see you go, love, and there's not many I'd trouble meself saying that for—you've always been such a good lodger, quiet, and no trouble, and regular with the rent, not leaving muck all over the bathroom like some of 'em—. I'm ever so sorry you had your things stole while you was here, I felt reely bad about that. It's not because of that you're going, I hope? You know, now the window's fixed it's not likely to happen again?"

"No, I'm sure it won't," Deborah said kindly. "No, it's just that I've got to earn some money somehow, I'm on my beam-ends."

"Tell you what, as you're goin' before your week, I'll give you part of your rent back. I don't 'ave to, you know, as I usually expect a week's notice, but in your case I will," said Mrs Tidbury handsomely, pulling a handful of half-crowns out of her apron pocket. "Because I was reely upset about the burglary."

"That's *ever* so kind of you," said Deborah, touched, laying a hand over the work-worn, swollen one, "but I don't think you should. You keep it and take yourself to the movies. I'd like you to. You've been very nice to me."

"All right, ta, then, ducks." The halfcrowns quickly disappeared again. "And I'll be thinking of you. Fancy teaching Carreen Gilmartin! Drop us a line to say 'ow you're gettin' on, won't you? Oh, I meant to tell you, now I come to think, there was a gentleman askin' for you yesterday. I was out last night and so I never see you to tell you."

"A gentleman? Did he give his name?"

"No, he didn't but he asked *ever* such a lot of questions. How long had you been here, and was this your first trip to England, and what did you do, and that; he seemed very nice-spoken, I begun to think he must be from one of them TV programmes. There wasn't any 'arm in tellin' 'im, was there? He was ever so sorry to hear about all your things bein' stole and your bad luck with the stories. Would it be a friend of yours, maybe?"

"I can't think who it can be. I haven't got any friends over here," Deborah said.

"No, that was what I told the gentleman. Would it be about a job, then?"

"The one I've got is the only one I'd applied for. He wasn't from the police—or Canada House? What did he look like?"

Mrs Tidbury proved unable to describe him. " 'E wasn't *tall,* but quite the gentleman. Had a raincoat on, and a hat . . ."

"Oh, well," said Deborah, "heaven knows who he is, but if he comes again, give him this address in Yorkshire. And I can be reached Care of Mrs Morne, at the Arundel Hotel. I'll write as soon as I know my plans."

"You do that, love. And if the job don't turn out all you 'ope," said Mrs Tidbury earnestly, "you come back 'ere, love, and I'll always be glad to put you up if I've a room. Bye-bye, enjoy yourself then, don't get mixed up with that there Slipper Killer in Yorkshire."

Deborah, running up the basement stairs, did not hear the parting remark, except for the word Yorkshire. "Goodbye," she called back, "hope you win your Dream House," and she began walking through the streets, with her rapid, extended stride, towards St Pancras Station, which was not far away.

Yorkshire, she thought. What will Yorkshire be like?

She tried to assemble fragments of information relating to Yorkshire from her reading of English literature. Something called Yorkshire pudding. York minster, Yorkshire moors. Of course, that was it. The Brontës, Wuthering Heights. Rock, heather, bog. Snow.

She shivered, and, having reached the station and learned

that there was a slow train at eight and a fast train at eleven with sleeping-car accommodation, she booked a sleeper and went to eat a meal in the station buffet and while away the time until she could go to her berth. Buying an evening paper she learned that colder weather was on its way with a prospect of sleet followed by snow in the northern half of the country.

She pulled out Carreen's paperback play and began to read it. Between bites of station hamburger she assimilated with growing puzzlement the fact that here was no callow, childish personality, to be swayed saplingwise by its mentors, even by two such determined mentors as Mrs Morne and Willie.

The intelligence that had given birth to this play was adult, mature, fully aware. How could Carreen Gilmartin be a thirteen-year-old in a red sweater and navy wool skirt, running away from her guardians? Was she a child at all? Or had she not really written the play?

But of course she must be a real child. There had been countless interviews in the press and on TV, articles, photographs, profiles, critical studies. It was unthinkable that any such deception could have been practised.

Glancing at her watch Deborah swallowed the last mouthful of brackish coffee and went to find her sleeper. What a wild-goose-chase this is, she reflected; how did I ever come to let myself be persuaded to take part in it? There was certainly something unusually compelling about Willie Rienz's personality. I don't think I like him, Deborah decided, locating her top bunk; although he is quite pleasant —well, I suppose Mrs Morne was quite pleasant too, but I definitely don't like her, I think she's sinister—I don't feel I could trust him. I shan't stay in this job. I'll go to Yorkshire, find Carreen if she's there, come back if she isn't, and then turn it in and go to the Consul for advice.

Unless there's something very special about Carreen.

Snuggling into warm red blankets she thought, Well, it's one way of seeing England, even if it is unwillingly on my part; and then realised it was a measure of the compulsive force of Willie Rienz's personality that he had persuaded her to go as far as this against her firm intentions. Another idea

flickered through her mind—Willie seemed very authorita-
tive for a mere public relations man?

Leaving the lower light on Deborah drifted into sleep
as the train began to move.

Her evening paper slipped to the floor and lay in a tossed
heap, its headlines resting cornerwise at the foot of the
washbasin: *Snow on the Way,* and, lower down *Escaped
Convict Aiming for Yorkshire?* "East Riding police have
been warned that Yorkshire-born 'Jock' Nash, escaped
homicidal maniac, may be heading for his home county.
The appearance of Nash, who committed the 'Lady's-
Slipper Murder' five years ago, is as follows . . ."

Later in the night Deborah woke. She had left the heater
full on and it was sending a stifling blast over her. She
struggled free of her blankets and switched it off. Outside
there seemed to be a gale blowing; she could hear the lash
of wind and rain on the metal roof just overhead, as the
train rocked on its way.

Sleep, once shed, was not easy to recapture; she lay in
feverish, clammy wakefulness, and the recollection of the
humiliating scene with the trio from Port and Bellingham's
swept over her in a scalding flood. She writhed again at
the memory of Mrs Morne's tacit assumption that she was
guilty but that it was of no importance. No one could work
for a woman like that! The queerest feature of the business
was that Mrs Morne, believing in Deborah's guilt, should
still want her as companion to a sensitive and gifted child.
Which Carreen certainly must be. And here was another
puzzle—how could the author of *To Crown the Unicorn*
bear to live in close daily contact with someone like Mrs
Morne? How could she have endured it for five years? And
what sort of a service would it be, now that she had apparently escaped, to help in her pursuit and recapture?

But perhaps Carreen had allies who would support her in
her flight from Mrs Morne and Willie. Deborah found
herself actively hoping so. Without noticing the process she
had ranged herself on the side of the unknown child. "I
have a chance to go away and I am going . . ." Perhaps
the uncle in Yorkshire was offering sanctuary. Willie had

said he was not on particularly good terms with Marion. But no, he was seriously ill . . . Deborah's eyes were beginning to close again. Her last thought was an altruistic wish on Carreen's behalf that whoever had taken her part was a person of weight and substance, able to stand up against Willie and Mrs Morne . . .

She was in a sodden, heavy slumber when the sleeping-car attendant woke her with a cup of tea and the news that they would reach Leeds in fifteen minutes. She struggled into her clothes, repacked her little case, and moved out into the corridor. The night was still black-dark, but above the horizon lay a reddish glow, against which she could see the uncouth, craggy outlines of factories interspersed with their tall chimneys. Plumes of whitish smoke blew raggedly south against the dark, and Deborah felt a cold nip in the air; even here in the heated corridor it was perceptibly colder than it had been last night.

She found the attendant and tipped him.

"Going on holiday, miss?"

"Not exactly . . . I'm going to a place call Herondale."

"Eh, you've a tidy way to go, still, then. You get the Cranton train at Leeds; joost across the platform when we get in. Yes, that's a pretty little place, Herondale. I remember going there once. You'll want to watch out for the Slipper Killer, though," he said jocularly.

"Slipper Killer?"

"Didn't you read in t'papers? Jock Nash, they call him the Slipper Killer. He cooms from soomwhere oop that way. Escaped from Broadmoor two days ago . . ."

"What did he do?"

"Eh, it wor soom crazy nonsense to do wi' a flower. Nash murdered a naturalist chap from Leeds University. He said this chap picked the flower as was noon of his to pick; joost a wild flower, it was, mind you. Then he was sorry about it, after: he fetched the chap all the way down to t'police station on his back wi' a broken neck, he made no attempt to deny he'd doon him in. But you can't have people going roond bashing chaps for reasons like that, can you? The joodge said he might take it into his head to repeat the offence. So they took and stook him in Broadmoor."

"Well I shall have to mind out, then, shan't I?" said Deborah lightly. "But I don't suppose I shall come across him. Anyway I shan't be picking any flowers. Goodbye, and thanks . . ."

The train slowed and stopped in the dimly lit cavern of Leeds station; as the man had said, her connection was waiting across the platform, a small, old, eccentric bit of rolling-stock in which she seemed to be the only passenger.

She selected a warmly fusty mahogany-and-velveteen carriage and had hardly sat down when the train rolled out with an immense hissing and grinding. A little dawn light was beginning to filter into the sky; she saw huge, illuminated multi-windowed buildings, all filled with machinery; endless black ranks of saw-toothed factory roofs, a great luminous clock-face that said ten past six. Then, as they left the environs of Leeds, sharply defined bony outlines of hills began to shoulder up against the clear, paling horizon. A cold, threatening landscape, already plunged deeper into winter than the soft south country she had left behind . . . Deborah wondered if somewhere out there a murderer was making his painful way homewards across those bleak and rugged hills; she felt sorry for him, out in the wild, stormy night, and wondered what sort of welcome he was likely to receive. But, as the attendant had said, you cannot commit murder for the sake of a wild flower, or where should we all be? He must be an unusual man, to feel so keenly about a thing like that.

Then with a fleeting chill she remembered that perhaps Careen, too, was out in that landscape, making her way towards Herondale. There had been no children visible on the train, and no Gilmartin on the sleeper-attendant's list of names, so if Carreen were really Yorkshire-bound she had either started earlier or chosen some other form of transport . . .

The little train came clanking to a halt in what appeared to be a totally deserted station. An unreadably small name-sign hung high up behind a small, dim, light-bulb—Glubley? Oakley? Dishley?

Deborah jumped out of the train and ran up to the guard's van. "Is this Cranton?" she called.

"Nay, luv, you've a way to go yet . . . Best coom oop here and keep warm."

And indeed the cold was bitter, she now noticed. Although it was still too dark to see it, she could feel the scrunch of ice under her feet on the paved platform. The rain must have turned to frost during the night.

She fetched her case while the train obligingly waited, and returned to the guard's cosy compartment. They clanked off again, and she was made benevolently welcome by the guard and fireman who were drinking tea laced with rum.

"Herondale, eh?" said the guard when they had asked and she had told her destination. "Ah, that's a pretty place coom spring, when the primroses is out; quiet, like, for a holiday at this time o' year, unless you're keen on fishing. But maybe you're not going on holiday?"

"Not exactly . . ."

"She'd best watch out for t'Slipper Murderer, eh, Sam?" said the fireman, winking.

"Don't you take any notice of him, luv; likely they'll have caught the chap by now, anyway. How are you going to get up to Herondale from Cranton, now? Is someone meeting you? It's a tidy step—all of twenty-five miles."

"Is there a bus?"

"Ah, that's the question," said the guard. "Soom days the bus roons half-way, as far as Leigh, oonce a week it goes right oop to Herondale, soom days it doosn't roon at all. But don't you worry, luv; we'll see you right. We'll inquire for you at Cranton."

And sure enough, when they reached Cranton, he abandoned his train, to vanish into the stationmaster's office, and came back triumphantly to say, "You're in loock, luv. There's a bus to Leigh in ten minutes, and I've phoned Bill Brigg, he has the taxi at Leigh, to meet you off it and take you on. Nay, no trooble . . ."

"I'm so grateful—" began Deborah confusedly, but he winked at her, called "Mind yersel' now—" and nipped back into the train, which was screeching for him impatiently. It rumbled off into the dusk of the morning, trailing a white plume of smoke over its shoulder.

Chilled and shivering, Deborah waited for the bus in the small station yard, speculating as to whether anywhere else in the world people had produced such amazing railway architecture. Cranton station might have been plucked straight out of some Gothic fairytale, so crusted was it with pinnacles, balconies, and canopies. It might be a hundred years old and was built of granite, plainly intended to last a thousand, despite the icy climate . . .

As the small country bus pulled up beside her Deborah began to wonder, rather forlornly, when she was likely to be able to get hold of some breakfast.

A winding road carried them up and up, through a landscape of pleated hills and small brisk rivers. They went featherstitching to and fro across the railway and a wider river, subsequently leaving the railway and striking up more steeply still across the wooded shoulder of a hill. Deborah noticed that the woods, unlike those of the South, had grass growing in them under the trees, and was reminded of the illustrations in an old Robin Hood book she had had as a child. But this was a menacing country: the stamp of armed Normans seemed a more probable sound here than the bugles of Robin's merry men.

The bus driver was an exception to Deborah's new-born theory that Yorkshiremen were a talkative, inquisitive, generously helpful race; surly and silent—perhaps he was hungry too—he sold her a ticket and urged his bus at a horrific speed up the twisting road, without showing any wish to know her business.

Deborah was glad to sink into her own silence and wait, hollow and sleepy and stiff, for the next encounter at Leigh; perhaps the taxi-driving Bill Brigg would know where food could be found, though the idea of shops or cafés in this bleak countryside seemed as out of place as sheep in Piccadilly.

Leigh turned out to be a neat, small town with half-a-dozen shops, hotel, and police station. Perhaps not unreasonably at eight in the morning everything was shut. But at the bus-station there was a round-faced, smiling little man who could only be Bill Brigg; he bounced over to the bus and helped Deborah out with her case, crying,

"Now doon't tell me you're not because I can see that you moost be the yoong lady from Loondon that Sam Oakroyd rang oop about. Very pleased to meet ye, and you want to go to Herondale, is that right? But first how about soom breakfast? You moost be clemmed if you coom oop on t'night train. Say the word and I'll take you roond to my missus and she'll have a pot of tea mashed in a twinkling."

Three quarters of an hour—and one massive Yorkshire breakfast—later, they were on the road to Herondale, threading their way up a steep-sided valley whose hills folded round more and more secretively.

"It's like Shangri-la," said Deborah, fascinated.

"Aye, it is that. It's a cut-off place, Herondale. Folks that lives there doosn't trooble their heads mooch about outside world. Who would you be visiting, then?" said Mr Brigg encouragingly. His sideways smile at her was as innocent as that of a child peeping at the Christmas parcels in a cupboard.

"Well," Deborah began cautiously. It occurred to her that the local taxi-driver would certainly know if an un-announced small girl had arrived to see John Gilmartin. "I don't actually know him but I'm on an errand to see Mr Gilmartin, at Herondale House."

"Eh—!" Mr Brigg's long-drawn exclamation had a shocked ring to it. "They'll not have told you, then? I doubt you'll not get to see him. Old Johnny Gilmartin's very, very ill."

"I did know he was ill," Deborah said. "Is it as bad as that? Actually I don't so much want to see him, himself, as to—you see, I'm working for his sister, Mrs Morne, and her ward, a little girl of thirteen, has possibly come up to visit her uncle, Mr Gilmartin, by mistake. I've come to take her home."

"I see." Bill Brigg's bright robin's eyes twinkled at her sidelong, implying that he was not such a fool as to miss the oddness of this story but that he was prepared to let

it pass. "Bit of a mix-oop, has there been? To the best of
my knowledge there's been no yoong lady oop to see Mr
Gilmartin the last few days."

"You know him, do you?"

"Old Johnny Gilmartin? Everybody knows *him*," Bill
Brigg said comfortably. "Wealthiest man in three counties
—for all he cares noothing for his brass. Aye, I've known
him since I was a little lad. Got bitten woonce by woon of
his dommed great Alsatians; aye, he gave me half a crown
to shoot oop about it. O' course he's given oop the dog-
breeding since he was taken badly—that used to be his
hobby, he took hoondreds of prizes. Aye, he's quite a
famous character in these parts. So you work for Mrs
Morne, do you? She used to have a house in Herondale,
but she lives in foreign parts nowadays, I believe? She and
old Johnny will be the only woons left of that family since
Mr Henry and Mr Laurence died. Foonny how the yoonger
woons went first; old Johnny was the eldest by a good bit.

"Now there's your first view of Herondale."

He had swung the car expertly round a bend in the road,
past a steep shoulder of hill sloping up to a formidable
crag, and he now gestured to a dark blur of trees two or
three miles farther up the valley.

"It's a quiet place, sure enough. But wonderful for birds.
And for the wild flowers in the soommer. There's folk
cooms from all parts of t'coontry to see the orchids that
grows here."

"Oh really?" said Deborah. "Is that why—wasn't it from
somewhere round here that the man they call the Slipper
Murderer came? That was to do with a wild flower, wasn't
it?"

"Aye, is that so? I'm not joost sure," said Mr Brigg
evasively. "But you yourself, now? You'll be American,
maybe?"

"Canadian," said Deborah, grinning at the familiar mistake. "This is my first visit to Yorkshire."

"Ah, it's a grand part. I hope you'll be cooming back
again. Mind, this isn't joost the best time of year for a visit.
Any time from now on Herondale's likely to be coot off—

it's not uncommon for this road to be drifted deep in snow and impassable for a coople of months in the winter."

"I'm not surprised," said Deborah, looking at the way the valley-sides came beetling down to the road. Steeply below them, now on the left, now on the right, a cider-coloured stream galloped among rocks. The sheerly angled fields looked hard and rough, as if only a thin skin of grass covered the underlying rock. Grey rocks pierced through the grass here and there, grey sheep the colour of the rocks grazed between them.

As they passed a cottage on the outskirts of Herondale village Deborah noticed that a wall, running straight uphill in the almost vertical field behind it, was exactly parallel with the thin wisp of blue smoke from the cottage chimney. A dog frantically barked on the end of a chain, and then sulked back into its kennel.

"Well, here we are," said Mr Brigg. The road had threaded between two paddock walls and a double row of chestnuts to emerge on a sizable village-green with houses irregularly placed round it. Not a soul was to be seen.

"Now, shall I take you straight oop to the House—that's a mile on beyond the village oop the hill yonder—or will you go to Mrs Lewthwaite's first?"

"She's Mr Gilmartin's housekeeper? Yes, I think that would be best—unless—won't she probably be up there anyway if he's ill?"

"True enough. Or—wait a minute, wait a minute, speak of the devil—there *is* Mrs Lewthwaite, just gone into her cottage," Mr Brigg said, as an aproned figure at the far end of the green came rapidly out of a gate in a wall and disappeared through a cottage door.

"Oh, that's fine, then. Well, thanks, Mr Brigg, you've been a wonderful help—if you'll just drop me at Mrs Lewthwaite's cottage . . ."

"And what about coming back?" he said, lingering when he had deposited her.

"I—I'm not quite sure when I'll be doing that. Probably in a couple of days. As Mr Gilmartin's so ill I'll probably stay at the inn," Deborah said, looking across the green at a solid, comfortable building with a battered sign which announced that it was the Trout Inn.

"Oh aye, Mrs Whitelaw will be able to put you oop . . . Well, if you're sure there's nought more I can do?" He was plainly rather reluctant to leave; obviously, thought Deborah, amused, he didn't feel he'd had his money's worth of gossip out of her yet. But she foiled his curiosity by waiting blandly, refusing to tap on Mrs Lewthwaite's door until he had thrown his car into gear and driven slowly away, stopping once to call back, "My number's Leigh 214—always ready to oblige when you want to go back."

"Thank you!" Deborah called, waving, and then she did knock on Mrs Lewthwaite's door.

There was a long pause before it opened. Deborah, standing solitary in the road, felt as if the unpeopled village-green behind her was bristling with eyes, as if she were being watched from the high valley-sides above the house roofs. In fact, when she turned restlessly to look, the green was still completely deserted and silent. Never, she thought, had she come to such a silent place. The small grey stone houses with their moss-grown granite roofs seemed secretively withdrawn into come conspiracy against her. Was that a face at a window? If so, the lace curtain flicked down again before there was time for a full glimpse. Deborah, town bred, was made uneasy by the silence; it seemed uncanny to hear no cars, no trains, not even the sound of an aircraft overhead.

She knocked again, more loudly, thinking, Don't they plough here? Don't they have tractors? Aren't there any birds? The distant lowing of a cow startled her so much that she almost jumped, and at the same moment, with a rattling of key in lock, Mrs Lewthwaite's door opened.

Deborah could see at once there was something wrong. The woman who faced her was pale-faced, sunken-lipped, and looked to be in the extremity of exhaustion—or was it fear? Her eyes were red-rimmed and the hand smoothing her apron was unsteady. Her grey hair had been hurriedly knotted into an untidy bun. But she had been a handsome woman once. Controlling her tremulous hands and lips she faced Deborah with dignity.

"Mrs Lewthwaite?" Deborah said. Remembering the housekeeper was deaf she spoke extra clearly.

"Yes?" The tone was guarded. "What can I do for you?"

"I've come on an errand from Mrs Morne—Mr Gilmartin's sister."

Mrs Lewthwaite's eyes swam with tears. "You can't see Mr Gilmartin, miss. He's very bad. The ambulance came two hours ago to take him to Cranton hospital. They say he's not likely to last the day."

"Oh my goodness! How—how dreadful. I'm very sorry."

Through the woman's obviously genuine grief Deborah could feel something like resentment against herself, an outsider, for intruding at such a time. But there was apprehension, too. What was Mrs Lewthwaite afraid of? Why did her eyes range nervously past Deborah's shoulder about the village-green?

"I hate to bother you just now," Deborah went on quickly, "but I just wanted to ask you if—if anyone had seen Mr Gilmartin's little niece, Carreen? It was thought she might have come up here to visit him; she didn't know he was ill, you see. I've come to take her home."

"Mr Henry's little girl, that would be?" A flicker of interest appeared in the drowned eyes. Whatever the woman had expected Deborah to ask, plainly it hadn't been this. "No, miss, so far as I know she hasn't been in Herondale. No one's been up to see Mr Gilmartin in the last few days. No one at all," she repeated assertively. "Was that all you wanted to know?" Her knuckles tightened on the edge of the door.

"Yes. No—wait. Is there anyone up at Herondale House now?"

"No, miss. It's all shut up and locked. I did that after the ambulance took him."

"You'll not be going back there?"

A sort of tremor passed through the woman but she kept her eyes fixed on Deborah's.

"No, miss. Not unless—unless he should recover, and

they say there's no hope of that. I'm tired out and nearly ill myself, I've not had a blink of sleep for three nights past. I'm going to bide at my own house awhile."

She looked at Deborah pleadingly, willing her to go away.

"Yes of course. You must be worn out. I'm only worrying—supposing the little girl were to arrive and go up to the house and find it empty?"

"Nay, that's not likely, miss. She'd have to pass through the village, wouldn't she? and likely Mr Brigg would be driving her up from Leigh; he or somebody else would be sure to warn her. News will have got all round the Dale by this afternoon."

"I suppose so," said Deborah, but still she hesitated, only half satisfied. The thought of the child arriving to find her uncle not there and the house shut up somehow haunted her. It had horribly familiar associations . . . "It's stupid of me, but I keep thinking of that man they call the Slipper Murderer—supposing she went up there on her own—I suppose there's no chance of his turning up around here—"

She stopped. A look of pure terror had come into Mrs Lewthwaite's eyes, her hand had flown to her mouth. "Oh, no, miss," she said quickly. "He'd never come here . . ."

"No, I suppose it's just a silly fancy of mine," Deborah said. "But I wonder—would it be possible for me to borrow the key and just go up and look at the house, maybe leave a note somewhere conspicuous?"

A guarded expression came into Mrs Lewthwaite's face. Her eyelids closed like shutters. "I couldn't undertake to let you do that, miss," she said flatly. "Not without permission from one of the family."

"If I telephone Mrs Morne and get permission? I imagine she'll be coming up here herself in a day or two to look after things—if—if her brother's so ill."

"Mrs Morne's his sister. She can do as she pleases," Mrs Lewthwaite said, exonerating herself from any part in the matter. "If you get leave from her it's nought to do wi' me. I'll give you a key, or Mr Bridie will; he's promised to feed the animals till other arrangements are made."

"Where does Mr Bridie live?"

"Yon cottage with the blue gate next to the Trout Inn."

"Can I telephone from the inn?"

"Yes. And now if you'll excuse me, miss," said Mrs Lewthwaite, definitely beginning to shut the door, "I'm off to my bed. I'm so tired I can hardly stand."

"Thank you very much for being so helpful," Deborah called through the rapidly closing crack, but her only answer was the click as the key turned again in the lock.

She walked across the green to the Trout Inn.

Two hours later Deborah was making her way up the rough track to Herondale House, in a mixture of triumph and apprehension.

When she had at last managed to get a call through to the Arundel Hotel, after a series of exasperating delays and false starts, Mrs Morne had been irritated that no news had been heard yet of Carreen, and imperative that Deborah should open up Herondale House and stay there. She received the news of John Gilmartin's dangerous condition with no apparent surprise. "If my brother's in hospital, Miss Lindsay, and the house is empty, it's certainly better that you should be there and look after the place—why, he has valuable silver, and first editions, and heaven knows what up there, waiting for someone to walk in and take what they fancy; yes, you go up there right away. I'll probably be coming to Yorkshire myself in a day or two.—No, there's no news of Carreen from Oxford or Devon. We've managed to keep it from the press up to now—so be discreet, will you?"

"Of course. You won't mind if I don't actually sleep at the House, will you? I'll spend the day there, but I'd prefer sleeping at the inn."

"No, I'd rather you slept at Herondale House," said Mrs Morne definitely. "If you're scared of being alone—" she sounded faintly contemptuous—"get Mrs Thingummy or one of the village women to sleep there with you." And she had rung off.

Deborah reflected that Mrs Morne seemed to have accepted Carreen's escapade with greater calm than Willie had expected. Perhaps the news of her brother's illness lessened Carreen's importance.

Mr Bridie had been perfectly prepared to part with the key of Herondale House, in fact almost eager to do so.

"To tell you the truth," he confided, "although I promised poor Mrs Lewthwaite I'd look after John's animals, I shall be quite glad not to; I'm having one of my wretched malarial spells, you know, not exactly incapacitating, but they make me feel out of sorts and mouldy. If a kind gel like you, Miss Lindsay, pops in and offers to stay up there and take the job on, I haven't the moral fibre to refuse." He smiled at her whimsically and Deborah forbore to mention that she hadn't actually offered to feed the animals.

"Tell you what," said Mr Bridie—he was an extraordinary-looking individual, tall, thin, and wispy, with fluffy grey hair and very bright eyes—"I'm expecting a call, so I can't stir out just now, but if you care to leave your case with me and have some lunch at the pub, I'll run you up to the House this afternoon in my old Rattletrap; that'll save you a walk; and then I can show you how to feed the beasts, and introduce you to Gelert—he's a bit touchy with strangers. And in the meantime I'll ask the good woman who does for me if she knows anybody in the village who'd be willing to spend a couple of nights up at the House with you."

"It's stupid of me to be scary," Deborah said, "but I've heard several bits of talk today about this Slipper Murderer and the idea's somehow got under my skin. He does come from somewhere around here, doesn't he?"

"Oh does he?" said Mr Bridie lightly and rapidly. "I don't keep abreast of the news much, I'm afraid. But of course you're quite right to be sensible—you look like a sensible gel, I must say . . . Now I'm sure Mrs Whitelaw will do you a delicious lunch . . ."

He ushered her towards the door of his stiflingly heated, brightly chintzy little cottage. Glancing through an open door Deborah was surprised to see a small, lavishly appointed conservatory with orchids and lilies and contemporary garden furniture. "Hobby of mine," said Mr

Bridie casually, following the direction of her eyes to the brilliant blooms. "Show you them sometime if you're going to be staying here a few days."

"They look wonderful."

"Nothing much." His tone was minimising. "Everyone round here's mad about flowers; plenty of rare specimens growing in the valley. Yes, you'll find the whole village is full of experts when you get to know the people here . . ."

Deborah could almost have laughed as his door closed gently but definitely in her face; it seemed so unlikely that any stranger would ever get to know the people in a village which, for all one could see of its inhabitants, might have been completely depopulated.

Mrs Whitelaw at the Trout, stout and rosy-faced but constrainedly silent, had indeed cooked a delicious lunch, and had left Deborah strictly alone with it, in the inn parlour, a pleasant, shabby room looking out on the green. Not a soul came or went while she was there, but she presently heard the racket of an aged car starting up, and when she went back to Mr Bridie's house later she found a note pinned to his door:

> *Miss Lindsay. So sorry, called to Cranton on urgent business, will take you to H. House on my return— one or two hours. R.B.*

Deborah, remembering the House was only a mile away, decided to wait no longer but walk up. Mr Bridie had her case and would no doubt bring it when he came—and she hoped too that he would escort some kindly woman who was prepared to share her vigil. She had spent enough time in this silent, scrutinising village—she was beginning to be unnerved by the total lack of human come-and-go. Besides, if she waited any longer the short afternoon would be gone, and she wanted daylight for her first reconnaissance of Herondale House.

She walked briskly up the steep, stony track.

The main road from Cranton to Leigh was marked A in the Ordnance Survey, but the traffic up and down it this dark November afternoon was hardly worthy of the narrowest unmetalled C. The small girl plodding along with her B.E.A. shoulder-bag had almost begun to despair of getting a lift, and the eight miles she had come, the seventeen more she had to go were beginning to weigh heavy on her. Although it was still a couple of hours to dusk the sky was thick and murky. On the steep valley-sides, above the scalloped edges of the fields, trees and scrub hung in an inky and menacing blur; Carreen could easily imagine little men with spears—Picts? Celts?—swarming down out of cover and taking her prisoner. Here and there what looked like a cave opened in the side of the hill: excellent lodging for Picts. And the steady rushing voice of the river in its rocky bed below would drown the noise of their approach till it was too late to flee . . .

Carreen told herself impatiently not to be a baby and stopped to adjust the pad of handkerchief on her blistered heel. The bubbling call of a belated curlew sounded close by and was cut off abruptly; then to her astonishment and delight she heard the sound of a car coming up the valley.

Firmly and confidently she stepped out into the middle of the road and waved.

The car—it was a rattly old Ford—came to a halt.

"Want a lift?" a voice called. "Where to?"

"Right up to Herondale if you're going so far," Carreen said.

"You're in luck. I'm going right there. Hop in."

She could see little of the driver in the dimness of the car's interior.

"You're a bit young, aren't you, to be hitch-hiking such a long way on your own?" he said. "Home for the school holidays?"

"Not exactly. A kind of holiday though," Carreen said politely.

"But hasn't your mother ever told you you shouldn't take lifts from strangers?" He carefully set his old vehicle in motion. "Supposing I was the Slipper Killer?"

"Who's he?" Carreen said.

"Never mind. Forget it."

"I'd spent all my money, you see, on a meal in Cranton.

42

So I couldn't get a taxi. As a matter of fact," Carreen said sedately, "I could tell you were a reliable kind of person from your voice. I'm quite a good judge of character."

"Are you indeed?" Her companion was quietly amused. "My last employer would hardly concur with your estimate of me."

"Oh? Why not?"

"He thought I was a super-tramp. And what he's saying now, having found that I've gone off and left him in the lurch, I shudder to contemplate."

"We show different facets of our personalities to different people," Carreen suggested.

"Gosh." Her companion sounded startled. "How old did you say you were?"

"I didn't say, but actually I'm thirteen."

"I see . . . Where are you at school?"

"Just now I'm not going to school. I haven't really got the time for it," she explained.

"How I sympathise. I used to have exactly that feeling, but it wasn't always easy to convince other people. In the end I was obliged to run away to sea. But how do you manage to avoid the educational treadmill?"

"Oh, I write plays," she said calmly. "I'm quite a successful playwright, so of course I'm allowed a good deal more latitude than most people of my age normally obtain."

"Of course . . . How very talented and ingenious of you. Now *I* never even thought of trying to write plays. My highest aspiration was to be a cabin boy. Have you written many?"

"Four," she said. "Four that have actually been performed, I mean. Of course a great many more childish efforts when I was younger. The last one put on was *To Crown the Unicorn*. I suppose you didn't see it by any chance?"

"I'm afraid not," he said regretfully. "To tell you the truth I've been right out of touch with current literary trends for the last four or five years. Four plays, indeed? By the age of thirteen? Dear me, you must have been working very hard."

"Yes, I have," said Carreen frankly. "Too hard, I believe. As a matter of fact I am running away."

"And coming to Herondale for a rest?" He slanted a glance at her sideways and took his eye quickly back to his driving in order to negotiate a small hump-backed bridge.

"I hope so. And you? Do you live there?"

"No. But I hope to," he said. "I can't imagine a pleasanter place to live. Specially if you're fond of farming. Or interested in birds and wild flowers. Have you been there before?"

"Yes, but not since I was very small. I can just vaguely remember the wild flowers—I remember my mother taking me to pick lilies-of-the-valley and telling me it was very uncommon to find them growing wild in the woods."

"All the more reason for not picking them." Her companion sounded mildly disapproving.

"Oh, we only picked a few . . . You know Herondale well?"

"Like you, I haven't been there for some years.—You were lucky to get this lift; it would have been a fairly long walk."

"At an average speed of three miles an hour," said Carreen, "I ought to have got there by nine o'clock tonight."

"Well, if I were your parents I should be worrying. After all, you couldn't rely on keeping up the average. Or on getting a lift. It's a lonely road."

"Luckily," said Carreen matter-of-factly, "my parents are dead so they won't be worrying."

"Oh, I'm so sorry. I wouldn't have said—"

"It is quite all right," she reassured him. "I minded very much at first, but five years have gone by and I have had time to adjust to the situation."

"In some ways I imagine it's an advantage to be an orphan," he remarked broodingly.

"You have parents?"

"Only a mother. And we haven't met for some time. We didn't see eye to eye."

44

"I should think parents can be very restricting," Carreen said reflectively, "if they try to hamper your activities."

"Or if *you* try to hamper *their* activities." He sounded oddly bitter, and Carreen tactfully did not pursue the subject, but concentrated on the view to her left, a high and frowning crag topping a steep slope of shale. It caught the last of the western light, and by contrast the road ahead seemed dangerously dark and shadowy. The driver switched on his sidelights.

"That's Blind Man's Crag," he said, nodding up at the cliff above. "There's quite a big cave up there. A Lady's-Slipper used to grow there, once. Someone took me to see it, a long time ago. I wonder if it's still there?"

"What is a Lady's-Slipper?"

"A kind of orchid. It's very rare. Big, with pinky-brown flowers."

"I don't know a great deal about English plants," she said politely. "You see I've mostly lived abroad. I have only just come back to England."

"Do you think you shall like it?"

"Probably," she said with her careful air of thoroughly digesting a subject before making a pronouncement. "The English seem to me a very considerate race, from what I have seen of them, far more so than the French."

"Considerate?" he said. "You really think so?"

"Oh yes. For instance, when I was walking through Cranton this morning I saw a notice stuck up in a house window on a postcard. It said 'Small doll lost, wearing Blue Dress. Apply With In.' That seemed to me a very *confiding* notice—obviously the person who had written it was quite sure that someone would take the trouble to pick up the small doll and return it."

"And you think that someone will?" he said musingly. "Small doll lost, wearing blue dress . . ."

"Oh, I'm quite sure they will. Now in France, nobody would bother."

"Well, let's hope you're right." He slowed the car to a crawl down a dangerously twisting little stretch of road. "Look, do you see those lights ahead up the valley? That's Herondale."

"My goodness, I am hungry," Carreen remarked. "I'm *starving.*"

It was the most childish remark he had yet heard her make.

"I hope they've got a good meal ready for you. Where are you staying?"

"With my uncle John."

"Are you?" he said on an unguarded note of surprise. "What a curious thing!"

"Why?"

"Because as it happens I too am going to stay with my uncle John. Would your uncle John's surname be Gilmartin, by any chance?"

"Yes it is. I'm Carreen Gilmartin."

"Carreen Gilmartin," he said reflectively. "Fancy that. I never even knew you existed. I suppose you must be Uncle Henry's daughter."

"Of course I am. Who are you?"

"I, my dear Carreen, am your cousin Jeremy Gilmartin, son of your deceased uncle Laurence."

"A cousin!" she said delightedly. "What an unexpected piece of good fortune."

"What brings you up into these parts, may I ask?"

"Well it's a long, complicated story," Carreen said guardedly. "Do you know my aunt Marion? She must be yours as well."

"I have that pleasure." His tone echoed hers. "But I haven't seen her for some years."

"Well, she—I—" Carreen halted and began again. "These plays I write—I mentioned them."

"Yes?"

"I began to feel that the situation in regard to them was something *unsatisfactory.*"

"Why? Is she taking all the cash and keeping you in penury?"

"Not, not exactly that," Carreen said vaguely. "I don't care much about money as a matter of fact. No, it was a rather *delicate, ethical* problem; I have been greatly exercised in my mind for a long time as to whether it would be proper to divulge it to a third party, but in the end I wrote to Uncle John about it. And he very kindly wrote back and invited me to visit him and discuss the matter when I came to England."

"So that is what you are doing. Did he offer any opinions?"

".Well, he *did,*" Carreen said. She looked at Jeremy doubtfully.

"But as it is a delicate, ethical matter and our acquaintance so far is very slight, you don't think it proper to divulge it to me. Very correct behaviour, my pretty little coz."

"Where does *that* come from?" she said, wrinkling her brow. "No, wait a minute, don't tell me, I know—"

"Just another successful playwright," he said teasingly.

She burst out laughing.

"So you have seen *some* plays?"

"Oh yes, in my younger days, before I shook clear of the educational system. And one precept I *did* imbibe, as I sat doggedly through school trips to the Comedies and the Histories and the Tragedies—"

"What was that?"

"Beware of relations! Wicked uncles, heartless aunts, usurping cousins, thankless daughters—Shakespeare's full of them. So *you'd* better watch out, sweet cousin."

"Do you know," Carreen said seriously, "I think I am going to find you very *congenial,* cousin Jeremy. I think perhaps I *will* propound my problem to you, after all."

"And get the opinion of the younger generation? I shall be honoured. I'll probably propound you some of my own in return. But," said Jeremy, "I've a notion that we're arriving, so you'll have to be succinct, or I shall be tantalisingly suspended in the middle of your interesting revelations." He frowned through the windscreen at a flickering view of stone houses disposed round a village-green. "Straight up there, if I'm not mistaken, is the track to Herondale House. Let's hope they've laid in plenty of fatted calf for the prodigals."

Deborah saw the chimneys first. The track zigzagged up the side of the valley, each bend a little steeper than the one before; at first she cut across the grass triangles from one section to the next, but then the gradient became too steep for that and she had to go round.

How do they ever manage to bring provisions up here in the snow? she wondered, gasping for breath. This road must become like iced stairs.

At last she topped the shoulder of hill; on the other side the track plunged steeply down again, there were trees, farm buildings, a high drystone wall, two big wrought-iron gates, and the house itself. It was large and silent, but she minded this silence much less than the silence of the village because she knew Herondale House was empty, whereas there she had felt eyes behind every windowpane.

It was a plain Georgian manor, square and unpretentious, with an added porch; both porch and house-front were trellised over with a wizened and leafless wistaria which softened the severe outline and made the house look harmless and untidy.

She unlocked the big outer door and found an inner glass-paned one leading to a small square hall with a staircase circling round three sides and stags' heads on the walls.

The house had a shut-in, individual smell of woodsmoke and coconut matting and potpourri and dogs; as Deborah stood hesitantly in the hall she felt as if she had stepped into the very aura of someone else's personality. It struck her afresh what an extremely queer thing she was doing: taking up quarters in the house of a dying man she had never met in order to wait for the possible arrival of a child she had never seen.

Where to begin? Heating, presumably. She found her way along a green-baize-barricaded passage to the large, dark kitchen. Depressed inspection showed that the solid-fuel stove was out and cold; doggedly, Deborah removed the top plate and started delving out handfuls of clinker.

Somewhere in the distance a dog howled furiously.

Having extracted a large bucketful of dead matter from the bowels of the stove, Deborah went in search of the ash-heap and some kindling. She found the back door along another dark passage, unbolted it, and discovered that it opened on to a cobbled courtyard. A tremendous crescendo of barks showed that this was where the dog lived. He came bursting out of his kennel by the back door and his chain brought him up raspingly within a foot of Deborah. She hoped that it was a strong chain—the dog was the largest police Alsatian she had ever met, and seemed willing and eager to tear her to fragments.

She found a woodshed and a chopper and kindling and coal. The stove lit sweetly, but all this had taken time, and although out of doors it was still light enough, inside the house the dusk was beginning to blur lines and veil corners. In the main rooms, which had been left curtained and shuttered, it was quite dark.

Deborah was washing her hands at the kitchen sink when the telephone startled her with its urgent shrilling in some distant and unexplored room. Tracking the sound to its source was like a mad obstacle race. Once, as a child, Deborah had been taken to see *The Cat and the Canary;* now, falling over shooting-sticks, opening doors that led into cupboards, barking her shins on unexpected steps, tripping over tigerskin rugs, she remembered the nightmare house in that film, and the hands that came claw-like from behind concealed panels.

"It's lucky I've got terribly strong nerves," she told herself firmly.

She found the telephone at last in a little cubbyhole beyond a room which, from the smell of old print and leather binding, seemed likely to be the library. By now it was too dark to be sure.

"Miss Morne?" said the voice in her ear unexpectedly.

"No, I'm Deborah Lindsay. I work for Mrs Morne," Deborah corrected.

"Of course, of course. How stupid of me. This is Bridie here—you came to my house earlier on. They told me you'd walked on up." (Who, she wondered?) "Miss Lindsay, I'm very sorry indeed—" Deborah's heart sank—"but I'm held up in Cranton and I'm not quite sure when I shall be able to come up to Herondale House."

"I see," said Deborah blankly.

"Don't worry about your suitcase. I'll see that someone. brings it up. I'm really telephoning to warn you—"

"Oh, yes?"

"—About the pump."

"About the pump," Deborah repeated.

"You will no doubt have lit the stove?"

"Yes, I have."

"Then it is necessary to make sure that the tank is full of water, otherwise a most regrettable explosion might occur."

"How do I find out?"

"There is an indicator on the house wall outside the back door. If it registers less than half full, start the pump at once."

"Where do I find the pump?"

"In the shed opposite the back door. It has a simple petrol engine—you are familiar with the kind of thing, I daresay? You start it by pulling a string. It may be rather dark in there by now," Mr Bridie said doubtfully. "You are equipped with a torch?"

"Torch?"

"A flashlight, you would say."

"No. But I've found some matches."

"Matches I should *not* advise . . . John sometimes keeps a torch in his desk drawer."

Deborah reflected that Mr Bridie seemed almost as familiar with the amenities—if amenities they could be called—of Herondale House as if he lived there himself.

"Mr Bridie," she said, "none of the lights will turn on. Can you tell me where the master-switch is?"

"Eh dear, that's another thing I forgot to warn you. He makes his own electricity—there's another little engine in the shed *next* the pump shed—quite a simple one, there should be no trouble about starting it. Don't forget to switch on the fuel supply first. And when you switch off, you cut off the fuel again, perfectly straightforward."

"Yes indeed."

"Then about Gelert."

"Gelert?"

50

"The dog. He is really a most harmless, good-natured creature if you approach him with confidence."

"I'm so glad to hear it."

"I had intended to bring up some bones for him, but in the meantime you will find a sack of dog biscuit in the pantry. There is also an ample supply of tinned dog food. I should be inclined to let the dog roam tonight; normally he requires a great deal of exercise and I fear he has been somewhat deprived of late."

"Poor thing. Mr Bridie—"

"—But what I *really* rang up to warn you about," he pursued—

"Yes?"

"Was that you should not neglect to feed the poultry and stock. You will find hens, geese, ducks, pigs, in various outhouses—"

"Oh, really?"

"There are some sacks of grain and pellets in the feed store."

"How shall I know which is which?"

"The names are printed on the sacks," Mr Bridie said patiently. "Layers' Pellets, Weaners' Mash, Farrows' Nuts."

"I see."

"On the whole I should advise you *not* to approach the goat."

"Goat?"

"He is confined in another of the sheds. A somewhat ill-conditioned animal," said Mr Bridie denigratingly.

"Mr Bridie, you will come up tonight and bring some-one to keep me company, won't you?"

"I will certainly do my utmost to come. In any case, have no anxiety about your bag. It shall be delivered without fail. But as to a companion . . . I fear that all the women in the village appear tied by family duties . . ."

"In that case," began Deborah resolutely. Then she broke off, listened a moment, and said, "Mr Bridie, what would a sort of loud thumping and bubbling overhead mean, should you think?"

"Dear me," he said, "I greatly fear that means there is very little water in the tank and that the boiler is beginning to boil, which means that you should start the pump at once in order to avoid a most dismaying explosion. Do not delay, my dear young lady. I will detain you no longer."

A click announced that he had rung off.

Goat, dog, hens, ducks, geese, pigs, two engines—I can't tackle all that, thought Deborah, it's crazy. I'm more likely to poison the animals and burn the house down. I'm leaving right now, I'll tell Mrs Lewthwaite that someone's *got* to come up from the village to see to it all. What right had the woman to go off and abandon it?

But then an extra-threatening rumble sounded overhead and she thought, no, I can't light his stove and then go off and leave it to burst the boiler . . . Flashlight in desk drawer, Mr Bridie said.

She fumbled her way across the pitch-dark room, letting out a sharp cry of fright once when her hand fell on something soft and resistant, rating herself for a fool next minute when she realised the object was a stuffed owl. Presently she found a drawer. Was this a torch—smooth, heavy, cylindrical? No, but oddly familiar, though she had never handled one before; she could not be mistaken, it was a pistol. A queer thing to keep in a desk drawer? No, sensible, if one lived as solitary a life as old John Gilmartin. With a surprising access of confidence Deborah took it out, not caring if it was loaded or not. And beside it was the torch—which cast a broad beam of golden light on mildewing brown bindings, jars of pampas grass (she had knocked one over) and the sparkle of black, uncurtained windows.

Rather hurriedly, feeling exposed, Deborah retreated across the library and found her way back to the kitchen. Outside the back door, keeping well beyond Gelert's ramping territory, she flung the torch-beam up the wall and found white-painted figures and a lead-weight indicator, dangling by a rope above the door. The weight hung perilously near the zero mark.

Now, the pump. She located two sheds and two engines. How could she tell which was which? The only solution was to try to start both. If possible. Deborah had never started anything more esoteric than an outboard before, but presumably all petrol engines functioned by the same principles? Forty pulls of a string later she was prepared to doubt this proposition, remembered, cursing, that she had forgotten to turn on the drip-feed, pulled again, and the engine came with insulting ease to life, throwing up a blaze of electric lights in half a dozen rooms in the house. Good, but the pump was even more urgent . . . Deborah began pulling doggedly at the string of the second engine, thinking with a corner of her mind, If the Slipper Killer turns up now I'll jolly well make him feed the goat.

At last the pump started with a coughing roar which changed in a moment to a regular chug-chug. The indicator began to creep comfortingly up the wall.

Gelert was still half throttling himself on the end of his chain, his salvos of barks now drowned by the pump.

Blow it all, thought Deborah, exalted by her success with the engines, we can't go on like this, he'll just have to kill me if he's going to. She had found the sacks of dog biscuit while searching for the pump, and she now approached Gelert with a double handful, and, quickly before terror could overcome her, unshackled his collar.

As might have been expected, he nearly knocked her down, putting his great muscular forepaws on her shoulders and lavishing her with licks from an eighteen-inch tongue.

"Gelert," she said accusingly, "I believe you're a fraud." Just the same she felt a faint prick of anxiety as he accompanied her lopingly to the henhouse, his great tail thrashing like the boom of a clipper ship, his muzzle never more than an inch away from her shins . . . Supposing she attempted to make off with some of John Gilmartin's silver cups— would Gelert have her run down and floored in half a second flat?

The ducks accepted their late feed with dignity, the hens went into a frantic cackling abandonment of fright at being tended by a stranger. Deborah found two eggs and trod on a third. The geese assaulted her hissingly with flailing wings, long weaving necks, and vicious beaks—but Gelert drove them off.

"You've upset your feed bucket and serve you right," Deborah shouted at them, and abandoned all intention of trying to shut them up again. They could serve as extra watchdogs if they were so anxious to make themselves unpleasant.

"Come on, Gelert, let's see if the stove needs more coal."

Now the light was on, the kitchen revealed itself as a big, pleasant room, its specklessly clean stone floor covered with bright rag rugs. White cupboards, check curtains, African violets in pots—it looked like a lived-in room.

The telephone rang again as Deborah finished stoking. Now she could find her way to it easily and realised that what she had nearly impaled herself on last time was a pair of rams' horns used as a hat-rack.

"Mr Gilmartin's house," she said.

"Is that Mrs Lewthwaite? Sister Dean at Cranton Hospital here. We are so sorry to tell you that Mr Gilmartin passed away half an hour ago."

"Oh my goodness," Deborah said blankly. "I'm—I'm dreadfully sorry. But I'm not Mrs Lewthwaite, she's at her own cottage. Perhaps you could ring her there—or Mr Bridie, if she's not on the telephone?"

"Mr Bridie is here, at the hospital. I will contact the Trout Inn. Thank you," the sister said, and rang off.

Deborah looked dazedly round the little telephone room. The bald, shocking news of death put her half-comic struggles in a different perspective.

I don't like it here in this house, she thought with chilly clarity. There's something wrong. Why did Mrs Lewthwaite go off and leave it, with all the animals to feed? She didn't look as ill as all that—she didn't look ill at all. She was just dead scared. If no one's coming up to keep me company I shan't stay—I'll get a room at the Trout.

Five minutes later she put the receiver down again with a sinking heart. Late November seemed an odd time to be redecorating all the inn bedrooms. Still, the end of the fishing season . . . no, it was probably rational enough. Gelert thrust a damp nose into her hand and she thought, Most people would say I'm making a lot of fuss about nothing. With a dog and a gun—where did I leave that pistol, by the way? On the kitchen table?—well, all right, I suppose there's nothing for it but to go upstairs and fix myself a bedroom.

If only I didn't feel that something disastrous had recently happened here.

The upper floor of the house was reassuring. White paint, floral prints, polished floors, worn but pleasant carpets—plainly John Gilmartin, though far from ostentatious with his wealth, had not despised homely comfort. Wandering about, up and down small flights of stairs, along irregular passages, Deborah located a bathroom, airing-cupboards, even radiators beginning to warm up . . . Opening a door at the head of the stairs, she found herself in a large bedroom which must, she reckoned, look out over the porch. It hardly needed the stripped-back bed, the various traces of occupation, to show her that this must have been John Gilmartin's room—she could feel it in the forlorn, abandoned atmosphere of a place recently vacated. A paraffin radiator still burned near the bed and the room was muggily warm.

The ambulance had come early that morning, shuttling its swift path up the zigzag track, stretcher-men had been quick and efficient—but just the same old John had died. What was the matter with him? Heart? Or something more malignant?

About to retreat quietly and rapidly from the room, Deborah stood still in sudden startled perplexity. Was the mattress—flung over the end of the bed—really soaking wet as it seemed? Was not that a large damp expanse on the blue fitted carpet, and all down the wall by the bed? She crossed the room and felt mattress, wall, carpet—they were all wringing wet. And the windowsill was blistered and swimming with water, the sash swollen, the ends of the curtains dark with wet . . . At some point last night, before the rain had turned to frost, this window must have stood open for—an hour, two hours, three hours? while the rain beat in on curtains and carpet and bed—and on the occupant of the bed? Was that why old John Gilmartin had had to be rushed to hospital first thing this morning? Because somebody had left the window open on him?

"You're having ridiculous, melodramatic fancies," Deborah scolded herself. "There's sure to be some perfectly rational explanation. Probably the window was opened after he had gone, to air the room . . . (But it hasn't rained all day). Well then, it wasn't rain at all, someone has been scrubbing everything within range of the bed. (But if you were washing the curtains you would take them down and wash them completely, not just the lower ends). Perhaps this wasn't his room at all," Deborah thought, ignoring the row of shoes and hunting-boots by the fireplace, and she tiptoed out, shutting the door behind her. Gelert whined at her side and followed with drooping tail.

Deborah found a smaller bedroom at the back of the house, overlooking the outhouses and cobbled yard, put sheets on a bed, hung a towel on an old-fashioned towel-horse. Returning to the kitchen she heard a rhythmic splash-splash outside the back door—the pump overflow? She looked up at the indicator and found that the lead weight had risen right to the top of the marks, and water was gushing from a vent pipe in the wall.

She had just switched off the pump and returned to the kitchen, wondering in a dispirited way whether there was food for humans as well as dogs and poultry in this house, when the front door bell rang.

For a wild moment Deborah debated with herself whether she had the moral courage to receive the caller, pistol in hand (which was what she felt inclined to do): then she remembered that of course it would be Mr Bridie or his messenger. She laid the pistol on the dresser, dropping a duster over it, summoned Gelert, and went to answer the door.

Two people stood outside, beyond the dark porch.

"I believe this is yours?" said the man, handing Deborah her case. "We passed a small boy at the bottom of the hill and he asked, as we were going up, whether we'd mind giving it to the young lady at the House."

"I see. Thank you so much." And so much for her hopes of enlisting the company of Mr Bridie's messenger. But who were this pair, then? Impossible to see much of them in the dark outside. "Won't you come in?" she said. "Can I—?"

"Thank you," the man said easily, moving after Deborah as she led the way into the hall. "We've come to see Mr. Gilmartin. He's expecting us, though not necessarily today."

"Oh, my goodness!" Deborah turned in dismay. "Hadn't you heard?"

She had her first view of him then. He was tall, thin,

young—but not, perhaps, so young as he looked. Black hair, high cheekbones, a pair of disconcertingly intelligent black eyes fixed on her in not altogether friendly inquiry; his clothes, though somewhat rumpled, were oddly elegant, but beneath the elegance he looked tough; more than tough; as if he could be—what was that word Willie had used of Mrs Morne?—formidable.

"Heard what?" said this formidable young man. "That Mr Gilmartin was ill? Yes, we knew that."

"He died today. The hospital rang up an hour ago."

"Oh, *no!*" The child in the background took a step forward, her eyes wide in horrified protest. "Not *dead?* Not Uncle John?"

The child's straight-falling dark hair just reached her shoulders; she wore scarlet mittens and cap, and a navy skirt.

Deborah said impulsively, "You're Carreen!"

"Yes. Why, how did you know? Are you Uncle John's housekeeper? Or a nurse?"

Carreen's clear-eyed assessing scrutiny was somehow uncomfortable.

"What did he die of?" the man said curtly.

"I'm afraid I don't know. I only arrived here a couple of hours ago myself."

"Then—if you don't mind my asking—who are you?" His voice was impatient.

"I'm—I work for Mrs Morne. Mr Gilmartin's sister. Actually I'm here to look after Carreen—and caretake the house till Mrs Morne arrives. My name's Deborah Lindsay."

Some unspoken communication flashed between the man and Carreen. A guarded, withdrawn look had closed over her face at Mrs Morne's name.

"Oh, I hardly think that will be necessary," the man said easily. "I'm Carreen's cousin, Jeremy Gilmartin. I'm going to take care of her interests from now on. But of course do stay till the morning, Miss—"

"Lindsay," Deborah supplied coldly.

"And we can talk things over. Mind if we dump our bags upstairs and find ourselves a couple of rooms?"

"Please," Deborah said with extreme politeness. "Obviously you must feel far more at home here than I do—and in a way have more right here."

"Why yes," Jeremy replied, turning to smile at her from the angle of the stairs—he had his aunt's trick, Deborah noticed, of smiling with the face but not the eyes—"why yes, in the circumstances, I think we have."

Deborah left them to sort themselves out upstairs and went into the kitchen—now warm as the result of her labours —to analyse her reactions. She stood staring at a store-cupboard handsomely equipped with tinned and packeted supplies, but did not really register what she saw.

She felt unaccountably furious.

She had been hoping that Carreen had found a champion, that Carreen would turn up safe and sound, and also that some stalwart person would arrive prepared to share the lonely vigil in Herondale House. All three hopes had now been fulfilled and here she was with a magnificent fit of bad temper. Why?

Because the other two did not need her, and felt they were the rightful occupiers while she was an interloper. Worse still, they plainly regarded her as a spy, sent by Mrs Morne.

Deborah told herself impatiently that she was being childish. What did it matter how two strangers regarded her? In any case it would be easy enough to put matters straight. She was tired, probably they were too, supper was the first essential.

Resolutely she found plates, peeled potatoes, and opened a couple of tins.

Then it occurred to her that she ought at least to telephone to London and report that Carreen was safe—and tell Mrs Morne of her brother's death, if the hospital had not already done so. Telephoning within earshot of the other two would be embarrassing, so it would be best to do it while they were upstairs.

Feeling unpleasantly furtive, she put through her call; waited impatiently during the usual hiatus of clicks, strange gabbling voices, and total silence . . .

"Arundel Hotel," said a voice loud and suddenly in her ear.

"Mrs Morne, please."

More delay. At last the voice reported, somewhat impatiently, "We have no Mrs Morne staying with us at present."

"You must have! She was with you this morning."

Further silence and delay. At last the voice admitted with reluctance,

"We did have a Mrs Morne, but she checked out this afternoon."

"Oh," said Deborah, disconcerted. "Can you tell me what her plans were?"

Pause, and mutter-mutter. "Our travel bureau supplied her with train reservations for Leeds, madam."

"I see. Thanks very much." Deborah rang off rather blankly.

Judging by the news, she decided, Mrs Morne must have heard of her brother's death, or at least of its imminence, and was losing no time in hastening to the scene. Was there something vulture-like about this? No, it was natural, of course; she must have been sorry that she did not arrive in time to see him. And doubtless there would be endless business connected with the funeral and the estate.

Jeremy came whistling downstairs into the kitchen.

"I brought a ham for my uncle," he said. "In the circumstances we might as well all have the benefit of it."

"It must have been a horrible shock for you, coming home and finding that he had just died."

"Something of a shock." The glance he gave her was swift and expressionless. "I knew he was ill, but not that he was as ill as that. He'd had the heart condition a long time.— Miss Lindsay?"

"Yes?"

"Carreen's been talking to me. She seems rather embarrassed at finding you here. I've gathered from her already that my aunt Marion has been exploiting her talents with a bare-faced rapacity which is quite in character, and Carreen hasn't the slightest intention of going back to the old arrangement. Marion must have despatched you to Yorkshire with even more than her usual lightning strategical insight, but there doesn't really seem much point in your mission, as things are."

"You don't seem very fond of your aunt," Deborah observed.

"I am not, very," he said drily. "We somehow have never hit it off. My father used to say of her—however you aren't interested in our family gossip. I think really your best course is to go back to her and tell her that Carreen proposes to live an independent life from now on."

Deborah was nettled by his tone of impatient authority. Who was he to give her orders about Carreen? "You forget that Mrs Morne is Carreen's guardian. And my employer. Obviously she has some say in the matter. Carreen is a minor."

"She's not her legal guardian. And any Court would take a more than doubtful view of someone who expected their ward to write a West End success every year," said Jeremy shortly.

"But if the child has a natural gift?"

"It ought to be naturally developed—not precociously exploited."

The fact that Deborah had been privately thinking exactly the same thing made it all the more annoying to have this arrogant young man laying down the law about it.

"Don't you think you are assuming a rather uncalled-for authority?"

"Someone's got to do it," he said tersely. "What beats me is how you can work for a person like my aunt Marion. Can't you see what she's like? Or does that sort of character appeal to you?"

"Anyway, how am I to know that you are Jeremy Gilmartin?" Deborah snapped, retreating hastily from an indefensible position. "Mrs Morne said she hadn't heard of you in years—where have you suddenly sprung from so handily? Have you proofs of your identity? You can't expect *me* to take you on trust. How am I to know you're not the Slipper Murderer, for example?"

Jeremy stood quietly for a moment, smiling his unamiable smile.

"A fair question," he said lightly. "Even if—to quote your own phrase—your assumption of authority seems a little uncalled-for. Why should I feel required to show proofs of my identity to *you?*—And if I told you where I had come from it would convey nothing and be impossible to substantiate. So shall we leave all this over for the moment?"

His tone and his raised eyebrows both called for some stinging retort, but as Deborah was about to deliver one he raised his hand admonishingly and said—"Here's Carreen."

They both fell silent as Carreen came into the room.

She had plainly made a detour to the library on her way down, for she carried an armful of calf-bound books.

"Uncle John must have been a delightful character," she said wistfully. "He has a most sympathetic library. I wish I could remember him better. I was only five on my last visit here."

"He was a misogynist and a martinet and he quarrelled with all his relatives," Jeremy said. "Otherwise he was delightful. Last time I saw him he said things about the whole family that would make your hair stand straight up. He was a master at the pulverising phrase; I shall never forget the time I took one of his duck-guns without permission. And of course he had a poor opinion of his sister Marion—as you probably know."

Everyone knows that, Deborah said to herself. So if you're trying to convince me that you have inside knowledge of family affairs, you'll have to do better than that, my friend.

"Shall I help you with the supper?" Carreen asked Deborah. "I have not much experience of cooking but feel confident that if you tell me what to do I can carry out your instructions."

"You could mash the potatoes," Deborah said smiling, and added, "I'm so glad to see that the skirt and sweater fit you."

"Oh! Did you get them? I thought they seemed too cheerful a choice for my aunt Marion. It was extremely kind of you."

"Not a bit," said Deborah. "After all, I was paid to." For the first time in about eighteen hours she remembered the shopping excursion to Port and Bellingham's and its unpleasant sequel. All that seemed very far away and unreal now. The work she had been doing for the last few hours —lighting fires, feeding animals, cooking—felt infinitely more substantial and important. "Oh my heavens!" she added, suddenly remembering, "there are pigs somewhere that I'm supposed to feed. And a goat. But the goat is said to be ill-conditioned."

"I'll feed them," Jeremy offered. "I had quite a bit to do with pigs during one phase of my existence."

"Oh, thank you. I discovered some sacks labelled Sows, Farrows, and Weaners," said Deborah, "but I hadn't decided which applied to which size of pig."

Jeremy took the torch and went out the back door.

"Jeremy doesn't look like the sort of person who would have associations with pigs," Carreen remarked, pushing back her fall of hair with a wrist as she mashed the potatoes. "He is a most exotic and glamorous cousin to encounter out of the blue. Just imagine! Before this afternoon when he kindly gave me a lift up from Leigh I had no idea that he existed."

"What!" said Deborah, considerably startled. "You hadn't met before?"

"No, never. That is what makes it so encouraging that he is prepared to take my part."

"Carreen," said Deborah, meeting the wide-set dark blue eyes squarely. "For some reason I seem to have got across to your cousin Jeremy (if he is your cousin Jeremy, she added to herself) on the subject of you and your aunt Marion, but I want you to know this: it's none of my business really, as I've only been working for Mrs Morne since yesterday and don't know either of you, but I think I'm on your side. I did promise I'd try and persuade you to go back, but I don't think your aunt should make you write plays if you don't want to."

"Thank you," said Carreen simply. "It is sustaining to know I have another friend. I was pinning my faith on Uncle John, you see, and felt somewhat unmanned when I learned of his death; I am sure Jeremy will be a vigorous partisan but he may not know all my aunt Marion's capabilities. And it is true that she has some claim to consideration; she has looked after me for five years."

"But perhaps if she can be brought to realise that you really don't want to write any more plays, she won't force you to? After all," said Deborah gently, "I don't see how she can *make* you."

"Is is rather difficult to explain . . . A great many people don't believe that I write the plays myself, and in a way I can see they are right. Lately I have been understanding this fact more and more, and I find the whole process morally wrong—I *hate* it!" she said vehemently. "I was ill, not long ago, and unable to write for a couple of months; when I recovered and Willie wanted me to start writing again—I found the prospect unbearable."

"How do you do your writing?" said Deborah.

"Well—it's like this: you see, I have always had a great many ideas and written them down, ever since I *could* write. Mummy—my mother—used to encourage me, but she avoided making a fuss about it. But Aunt Marion and Willie concentrate on me to an *inordinate* extent—particularly Willie—and oblige me to discuss my ideas and be explicit about them, and then Willie makes suggestions for their development which are difficult not to adopt—until in the end I am in a state of confusion because I can see that my original idea has been transformed in a way quite beyond my own power to achieve, and yet there is no clearly marked or distinctive dividing line."

She looked up, smiling but troubled, and Deborah felt a warm surge of protective affection.

"And you feel that your ideas are being unfairly exploited?"

"It is not so much *that*," Carreen explained, "after all, ideas are common property. But I feel the public are being exploited. They apparently are glad to pay to see plays by a person of thirteen—I find this absurd in itself but one must accept that most people are sadly irrational—and their money is being taken on what amounts to false pretences. I *detest* feeling that I am associated with this."

"Many people would feel that you are being unnecessarily scrupulous," Deborah said fairly. "After all, the original ideas are yours. Think how many hands go to writing a film script."

"Still, I detest it. And yet I do have obligations to Aunt Marion. She has looked after me since my parents died. Moreover, recently some of her investments have gone wrong and she has had severe financial worries."

She doesn't give that impression, Deborah reflected. Could the financial worries have been invented by Aunt Marion as an extra bit of moral blackmail? It seemed not unlikely. She said,

"Well, I think you've got a perfectly valid case, and I'm sure we can put it to your aunt. After all, it's probably not as if you wanted to stop writing for good."

"Oh, no *indeed*," Carreen said earnestly. "When I am fully grown I intend to do little else. But it is also necessary to gather a great deal more material. If I write too much now I may suffer from insufficiency later."

But not from poverty of expression, Deborah thought, chuckling a little inwardly as she opened another tin of peas. Carreen was not at all what she had expected. Although obviously intelligent and sensitive far beyond her years she seemed to have remained curiously innocent and, in a way, young for her age—a strange anomaly in someone brought up by two sophisticates like Mrs Morne and Willie. That at least might be laid to Aunt Marion's credit. The result was very attractive and likeable, whatever the cause.

Jeremy came in looking cross.

"Did the goat give trouble?" Carreen inquired.

"No. But the pigs spilt cod-liver-oil over my suede shoes. And it's getting infernally cold. We shall have snow if it goes on like this."

While they were eating supper in the kitchen Carreen suddenly exclaimed, "Who's that?"

She was facing the uncurtained window, the other two had their backs to it. But when they turned round there was no one to be seen.

"Perhaps they knocked at the door but couldn't make us hear," Deborah suggested, and went to see. But there was nobody outside. At this moment a loud angry clamour broke out among the geese in the field beyond the henhouse.

"Who did you see, Carreen?" Deborah asked, returning.

"A man—I had no more than a very quick glimpse of him. He looked a bit like cousin Jeremy."

"Who the devil could it have been?" Jeremy wondered.

Deborah, who had had time to laugh at her earlier fears, said, "Probably some neighbour taking a local right-of-way past the house and peeping in to see who's here. The dog hasn't barked, so it can't be a stranger."

She stooped to pat Gelert, who was in a blissful doze with his back against the stove and his chin resting on the hambone.

"Just the same I'll check on the door and window fastenings," Jeremy said. "It's probably known from here to Cranton that Uncle John has died, and some opportunist might have decided this was the moment to grab his silver."

While he went the rounds the other two washed the dishes. They had almost finished when all the lights suddenly went out.

"Blow!" said Deborah. "What can have happened?" She noticed that the gentle chug-chug of the generating engine had stopped. "I wonder if anyone's been fooling with it?" She picked up the torch and started somewhat nervously for the back door. Carreen said, "I'm coming too."

"Hi!" called Jeremy's voice from the stairs. "What's going on?" He caught them up. Deborah thought he looked very pale—or was it the effect of the torchlight?

"We don't know," she said lightly. "I wondered if someone had been fiddling with the generator. It's stopped. We're just going to see."

"Better let me."

In the end they all went. Jeremy inspected the engine and said, "Who started it? Was it you?"

"Yes. Why?" Deborah was faintly irritated by his tone. "Aren't you used to these things?"

"No, I'm not, as a matter of fact. What's the matter?"

"Only that it has two fuel supplies. You start it on petrol and then switch to diesel fuel. You left it running on petrol, and now it's used up all the petrol supply and we shan't be able to start it again till we get some more."

"Well I'm sorry," said Deborah crossly, "but how the devil was I supposed to know a thing like that?"

"I should have thought you'd have the sense to notice the two different fuel tanks," Jeremy said exasperatingly, "but I suppose the female mind always boggles at the simplest bit of machinery."

While Deborah and Jeremy stared at each other stormily, Carreen alone remained tranquil. "Surely it is of no importance?" she said. "I noticed a plentiful supply of lamps and candles in the room next the kitchen and feel convinced that we can manage with those till morning—unless the petrol from your car would start the engine, cousin Jeremy?"

"Wrong kind, duck. Never mind, worse things happen at sea," he said, and shepherded them indoors, carefully relocking the back door behind them. They found and lit the oil-lamps.

"I think it was *extremely* clever of you to have started that engine all on your own," Carreen said to Deborah, who was still looking ruffled. *"I should have been helpless in such a situation."*

Deborah suddenly burst out laughing and tousled Carreen's hair. "Thank you," she said. "I don't really need soothing down as badly as that, but it's been a long day. I'm for bed, I think. Where are you sleeping, Carreen?"

"In a room next the one which I think is yours. I too am going to bed. I sat up in a slow train all last night and listened to the conversation of an old lady who told me all about her nine children."

They took a lamp with them. As they reached the head of the stairs the telephone rang.

"Keep the lamp, I know my way in the dark by now," Deborah said to Carreen, and ran down again.

It was Mrs Morne. "Miss Lindsay," said her high, irritable voice. "I'm ringing from Leeds. Is there any news?"

"You—you've heard about Mr Gilmartin?"

"Yes, yes, we had a wire. That's why we came north.

We'll be in Herondale early tomorrow. I meant about Carreen?"

"Yes, she's here. With Mr Jeremy Gilmartin."

"With *whom?*" Mrs Morne's voice was sharp with incredulity.

"Her cousin Jeremy."

"Laurence's son? But he's been missing for years! Where did he come from?"

"I don't know, Mrs Morne."

"Well, what does he want?"

"I think he had been intending to visit his uncle. He didn't know Mr Gilmartin had died."

"Did he see John? Before he died?"

"No, I don't think so—no."

Suddenly and rather unnervingly, Deborah became convinced that there was somebody near her in the dark. She was sure she could hear breathing. It was a very unpleasant sensation.

"Is he there? At the house? With you and Carreen?"

"Yes."

"How can you be sure it is the real Jeremy and not some impostor?"

"He looks rather like you," Deborah said doubtfully.

"Well tell him I won't have him sleeping at the house! If he's the genuine Jeremy—which I very much doubt— he'd better go to the Trout. They'll know him there. We'll be arriving there tomorrow."

"Oh, I don't think they—"

But Mrs Morne had rung off.

Deborah stood listening in the dark, desperately conscious of the thump of her heart. But the sensation of somebody close beside her had gone, must have been imagination, and she made her way back along the corridor to the ray of lamplight shining from the kitchen door. Jeremy was sitting in the kitchen, placidly reading the local paper.

"I suppose that was my aunt Marion?" he said, raising his brows. "And no doubt she told you that she wouldn't have me in the house?"

"Well—yes, she did," Deborah said hesitantly.

"So what are you going to do about it?" He smiled at her, with annoying tranquillity.

"Nothing," Deborah said. She found to her own surprise that she was quite definite on this point. In spite of her doubts about Jeremy she much preferred his presence to being alone with the young Carreen and a possible prowler in the grounds outside. "You couldn't stay at the Trout anyway. They're redecorating."

"And you won't condemn me to sleeping with the goat? Considerate girl."

She refused to be drawn.

"I daresay my aunt would, she's quite capable of it," he said broodingly. "But she wouldn't have a leg to stand on, as it happens. Just wait till she finds out what I know."

"Yes?" said Deborah, remembering what she had come for—the duster on the dresser—and stretching out her hand to pick it up.

"Yes." Jeremy gave her a bland smile. "I know the main points of Uncle John's will. You look surprised?"

Deborah was not showing surprise at his statement—though it did give food for thought. What worried her was that the pistol which she had concealed under the duster a couple of hours ago was no longer there.

She said, "Mr Gilmartin, did you find and put away your uncle's pistol? I'd like to borrow it for the night if you don't mind."

His eyebrows shot up. He said, "Certainly I've no objection if you feel happier that way. But I took no pistol. Where was it?"

"Here. Under a duster."

"Never touched it. Perhaps Carreen—"

"I hardly think so. Pistols don't seem exactly her line. But I'll ask her."

Carreen disclaimed all knowledge of the pistol—nor did any amount of searching reveal it. Jeremy seemed sincerely puzzled and concerned—but Deborah couldn't help feeling that he took the disappearance rather more lightly than was justified.

Who could have got it? Did Jeremy guess? Could somebody have slipped in—somebody who had been watching earlier through the kitchen window and seen where she hid the gun? Had the back door been left open when they all went out to look at the engine?

Deborah went slowly upstairs with these unanswered questions gnawing at her mind. If someone from outside had taken the pistol—as they must have unless Jeremy or Carreen were lying—where was that someone now?

An icy, knife-like draught blew along the landing from John Gilmartin's open bedroom door. Surely she had shut it? Carrying a lamp she went to investigate and found the big centre window open. Cold wind was blowing over the bed, as it must have on the previous night. Chilly and trembling, Deborah shut the window, noticing that the catch was faulty. The window opened over the porch; it would be easy to climb up the wistaria and get in that way. Or out. Or—conceivably—to open the window and leave it like that as a signal?

Deborah went to bed. She locked her door, after putting her head into the room next door and advising Carreen to do the same.

Dawn next day was late and dark and heralded only by the sound of cocks crowing, near and far. Deborah, used to the cheerful hurly-burly of London, found this chilling and lonely, though poetic; she flung on a coat, unlocked her door, and tapped on Carreen's.

"It's me, Deborah."

She heard Carreen patter across and unlock.

"Hullo. How did you sleep?"

"Beautifully, thank you. But I had to allow myself two extra blankets during the night. Look at that frost!"

It lay thick as crystal and grey under a lowering sky on the fields beyond the house. To the right, the valley dropped steeply away: they could see the line of the river, with a field on either side, the trees that shrouded Herondale village, and then the steeper climb, tier on tier, of the hills across the valley.

"Your aunt rang up last night," Deborah said. "She's at Leeds, coming over to Herondale this morning. She means to stay at the Trout, but I don't know if they'll be able to have her; they told me they were redecorating. In which case I suppose she'll want to come here. There are several empty bedrooms." Not counting the one over the porch, she thought.

"Then I must summon my moral courage to face her." Carreen looked anxious but resolute. "In fact I see now that it was a most childish piece of self-indulgence to run away, but I was unnerved by the problem of what to say at the press conference."

"Well, let's get dressed and make some breakfast. You'll feel braver after that. I only hope the stove has stayed in. And that the hens have laid a few eggs."

Deborah finished dressing first, wishing that the clothes she had left were more adequate for the Yorkshire climate, and went down while Carreen was still searching for a case containing some things of her mother's which had been left in an attic at Herondale House some years ago.

Jeremy came in as Deborah reached the kitchen. He carried a bowl of eggs and a handful of goose-feathers.

"Did you let the geese out last night?" he asked.

"They got away from me," Deborah said guiltily. "I'm terrified of geese."

"Not quite the country type, are you? As a result a fox has got one. These are all that's left."

"Oh, heavens, I'm terribly sorry—"

"Forget it. After all," said Jeremy coldly, "Uncle John won't know, will he?"

Deborah looked at him in angry silence.

After breakfast Jeremy departed in his ramshackle car, saying that he was going to Cranton hospital to make the funeral arrangements and would then visit his uncle's lawyer Mr Proudshaw; did Carreen want to come? Carreen, looking rather wan and pinched, said she would prefer to stay behind with Deborah, if Jeremy would promise to be back in time for Aunt Marion's arrival.

"I'll be here, duck, don't worry," he said, giving her a quick smile. Deborah had to admit to herself that, though she herself had plenty of mental reservations about Jeremy Gilmartin, there was something very nice about the way he treated his young cousin. Carreen obviously adored him already.

"Goodbye, Miss Lindsay," he added with frigid courtesy. "I've fed the pigs and the goat; I'll attend to the rest of the poultry when I get back so you needn't worry about them."

"It isn't the slightest trouble." Deborah's courtesy equalled his, she hoped. "Unless of course you think I'm likely to poison them?"

He shrugged and went off to his car, pausing to call back, "I'll lay in some new engine fuel too."

"Bother," said Deborah when he had gone, "I should have asked him to buy bread in Cranton. There may be a shop in Herondale but if so I didn't see it."

She rang the Trout to inquire about rooms for Mrs Morne but found she need not have bothered. Mrs Morne had called up herself from Leeds the previous evening, and had somehow coerced the Whitelaws into finishing their decorating overnight; she had booked rooms and was expected to arrive at noon. The three from Herondale House were invited to lunch at the Trout with her and Mr Rienz.

At half-past twelve Jeremy still had not returned, so Deborah and Carreen tied up the reproachful Gelert and walked down the zigzag track to the village.

"I wish I were not such an *abominable* coward," Carreen said sighing.

Deborah said, "I read once that the best way to cure yourself of cowardice is to do something really shocking— like going to the Ritz with your own watercress and golden syrup in a tin, and asking for a plate of plain bread-and-butter."

Carreen began to laugh helplessly. "What a wonderful idea! But Aunt Marion is so much more formidable than the Ritz."

"Just think of her as a problem in plotting," Deborah suggested.

"Yes, that is what I must do. I wonder why some problems are interesting and stimulating, while others paralyse one with alarm? Deborah, I am *extremely* glad that you are with me."

She stuck her arm confidingly through Deborah's, who

found herself absurdly touched, though she had to battle against a guilty sensation of disloyalty to Mrs Morne.

"I'm glad too, honey," she said.

"It was—unexpected—of Aunt Marion to pick someone like *you* for my teacher," Carreen went on.

Deborah couldn't have agreed more. Not for the first or the second time she wondered what had possessed Mrs Morne to choose her, out of all the applicants, to be Carreen's companion. Since being given the brush-off by Patrick she had become diffident and humble in her approach to the rest of the world; her naturally warm-hearted, friendly temperament had received a severe check and she no longer met strangers in the happy and unquestioning faith that, because she found other people endlessly absorbing and worthwhile, they must necessarily feel the same way towards her.

It seemed to her that there must have been many more suitable candidates for the position of Carreen's mentor.

"What sort of teacher did you expect?" she asked cautiously.

"Oh—someone kind of middle-aged and—*flabby*," Carreen said with distaste. "Like Mademoiselle Jadoux who used to teach me French. She was all shrivelled up and soft, like a last-year's apple, and scared to death of Aunt Marion. I think Aunt Marion likes people that she can push around. But you don't look pushable. *Are* you?"

"Well," Deborah said laughing, "I let myself be pushed up to Yorkshire to look for you, didn't I? So I suppose I must be."

"Ah, but you hadn't heard my side of the case then. Why did you apply for the job, anyway?"

"Because I needed the money. I'd had all my things stolen."

"*All?* Goodness," said Carreen, turning to look at her with wide-eyed interest. "How extremely exciting and dramatic. Though very upsetting. No wonder you wanted a job."

"And I must say I was curious to know what you would be like, when I found that it was you who were to be my pupil."

"I expect you thought I would be horrible. Most people do," Carreen said simply. "Really it was brave of you to take the job on when you found out."

"I did try to back out," Deborah admitted. "But your aunt——" Her voice trailed off. She found that she could not talk about the episode of the necklace. Carreen, however, appeared to guess the sort of thing this reticence concealed, for she gave Deborah a quick rueful grin.

"Aunt Marion puts pressure, doesn't she? Sometimes in pretty mean ways. People like you—with principles, I mean —always get the worst of it against people like my aunt Marion because she doesn't have any scruples about the methods she uses. You must take care never to let her get a lever-hold on you or she'll use it as much as she can. Do you think it's horrible of me to warn you like this?" she added candidly.

"Not horrible—honest." But suppose, Deborah thought, Mrs Morne already had a hold—what use would be made of it?

She glanced in some compunction at the child beside her going forward so valiantly to the assignation at the Trout Inn. How difficult was it going to be to take her part against her aunt?

"Jeremy is the most courageous of us when it comes to braving Aunt Marion, I suppose," Carreen said sighing. "But then he has no obligations and nothing to lose."

"He doesn't trust *me* much," Deborah remarked irrelevantly.

"Oh, that is probably on account of his unhappy childhood," Carreen said with a sage air. "He has told me a little about it. He views all women with a prejudiced eye because of his mother, who, I must say, sounds a most miserable individual. I should not let yourself be intimidated by his manner."

Deborah could not help laughing at this, and so they came cheerfully into Herondale village.

The green was still shrouded in quiet and emptiness. But as before Deborah had the sensation of eyes behind every lace curtain as they passed.

"There's something *wrong* with this place," she exclaimed. "Surely it's not natural to be so quiet? I wonder what it can be?—But maybe I just don't understand English country life."

A huge Daimler stood in front of the Trout Inn. Their fears of the coming interview seemed to have been groundless, they discovered: Willie Rienz met them at the door, said laughingly, *"Here's* our runaway at last," pulled Carreen's ear in the most friendly manner, and led them into the parlour.

Mrs Morne at the Trout, correctly dressed for the country in tweeds and pearls, gaily and graciously dispensing sherry for Deborah and ginger-ale for Carreen, seemed a totally different personality from the shrewd, weary businesswoman at the Arundel Hotel. She teased Carreen about her escapade—making it appear that the whole thing was unnecessarily melodramatic, indeed, that Carreen had totally misunderstood her aunt's attitude—congratulated Deborah on finding and looking after Herondale House, and inquired mockingly as to the whereabouts of Jeremy.

"This young man who says he's a Gilmartin! Of course I don't wish to be captious, but, well, if he *is* what he says he is, there's a name for people who don't bother to keep in touch with their relatives until it's time for the will to be read, and it's not a very nice one." She laughed, melodiously.

"Oh, *no,* Aunt Marion, he isn't in the least that kind of person I assure you," Carreen said earnestly.

"Don't wear yourself out trying to uphold my reputation, little coz, it will just have to lurch along by itself."

Jeremy stood in the parlour doorway, looking cool and ironical; he gave the company a little bow and his black eyes narrowed reflectively as they met those of Mrs Morne.

"Jeremy, my dear boy! What a pleasure!"

"I'm so glad we remember each other," he said agreeably. "If we do?"

"Of *course!* Of course we do!" Mrs Morne beamed at him. "And now, what will you have to drink? And I don't believe you have been introduced to Mr Rienz, who looks after Carreen's little affairs, have you?"

"I don't believe I have," Jeremy agreed. "Talking about

Carreen's little affairs, I hope I can make it plain that I feel she has an absolute right to—"

"My *dear* Jeremy, I assure you there is no need for that *militant* expression. I've just been telling this silly girl that she's been making an absolute mountain out of a *molehill*. If she feels—wisely I am sure—that she needs a rest from writing for a couple of years, I should be the *last* person to suggest otherwise. You should have known *that*," Mrs Morne said, smiling brilliantly at Carreen. "You have a rest, and learn some arithmetic and spelling—*never* your strong point, my love—which clever Miss Lindsay will teach you." The smile extended to Deborah and Mrs Morne added, "By the way, Miss Lindsay, in your amazingly speedy and efficient departure to Yorkshire you left *this* behind. I knew you wanted to give it to Carreen, so I brought it along." She handed Carreen a gaily wrapped package, saying lightly, "A gift from your new teacher, Carrie. Mind you work hard for her."

Jeremy's eyes came round to Deborah's face and stayed there thoughtfully as Carreen opened the box and exclaimed in delight at the green-and-silver necklace. Deborah studied the tightly interlocked fingers in her lap, biting her lips for control. All her former feelings for Mrs Morne came flooding back. How could one work for such a woman? But if Carreen needed someone to stand by her . . . But if Mrs Morne really intended to be so graciously complaisant about the playwriting . . . If Jeremy . . .

Jeremy was saying, "Fine. Well, if we are all agreed about Carreen's future, may I talk for a moment about other arrangements? The vicar suggests tomorrow afternoon for the funeral, Aunt Marion—he's afraid there's snow on the way and a lot of the mourners will have long distances to come —and Mr Proudshaw is coming up this evening to read the Will. Would you prefer him to do it here, or at the House?"

Mrs Morne looked slightly—very slightly—put out. "Dear Jeremy, how busy you have been, how efficient. Was it really necessary? I came perfectly prepared to undertake these painful duties. For someone who has been out of touch for so long, you show a *surprising* grasp—"

"Out of touch with *you*, dear Aunt Marion," Jeremy said blandly, "but less so with Uncle John. Perhaps he had not told you that? Now, as to the will-reading—"

"Oh, let's have it here. Here, by all means. I've detested Herondale House ever since I was a child. I shall lose no time in putting it up for sale."

"—I think Mrs Whitelaw wants to tell us that lunch is ready," said Jeremy.

"And now, my dear boy," said Mrs Morne, as Willie carved the duck, "I want you to tell us *all* about your tremendously exciting life."

Jeremy looked benevolently amused. "Not a bit exciting, dear Aunt Marion. After I decided I didn't like my mother's third husband any better than the second and ran away to sea (running away is evidently quite a Gilmartin family trait, didn't you run away once, Aunt?) it was just one freighter after another, until I jumped ship in Hull this week. Nothing like so exciting or dangerous as that time when I borrowed Uncle John's duck gun without his permission."

"Did you do that?" Mrs Morne looked vaguely disapproving.

"When I was twelve. But perhaps you have forgotten the episode."

"I'm afraid I had, my dear boy. Now, Carrie my love, if you have finished your coffee, can you let us know whether you want to stay down here with us at the Trout, or go back to roughing it at the House with Jeremy and Miss Lindsay?"

"Oh, the House, please," said Carreen decidedly. "I have not nearly exhausted the resources of Uncle John's library."

"Then Willie had better bring the rest of your clothes up this afternoon—you went off without them, silly girl."

"And I ought to be getting back," Jeremy said. "I noticed the drystone wall is broken at the end of Uncle John's garden—somebody's heifers from the pasture beyond will be breaking through and wreaking havoc if it's not mended pretty soon."

"Dear Jeremy, you missed your vocation going to sea; you should have been a land agent." His aunt gave him her sweetest smile and he smiled back seraphically.

"Dear Aunt Marion, thank you for the delicious lunch; it has been such a pleasure to see you again."

"That boy has changed out of all recognition—and *not* for the better," Mrs Morne said discontentedly as Jeremy and Carreen strolled out on to the green. "I find something decidedly sly about him. It seems a *remarkable* coincidence that he should have turned up just now." She gave Deborah a chilly smile and added, "No doubt he appears full of charm to you; Carreen is plainly bowled over by him. But I should take him with a grain of salt, Miss Lindsay."

Deborah murmured polite thanks for the lunch and moved after the other two.

"I want to call on Uncle John's housekeeper and ask when she can come back," Jeremy said as she joined him.

"She told me yesterday she needed a thorough rest," Deborah remarked doubtfully. "She'd been nursing him day and night, I gather. But maybe you can persuade her. She lives in that little house over there."

He nodded and moved off; however when they reached Mrs Lewthwaite's house they found a card tacked to the door which said, *"Out all day. Please leave bread with Mr Bridie."*

"Funny," said Jeremy, "I could have sworn I saw someone peering at us through the curtain as we crossed the green."

"A trick of your imagination," Carreen suggested. "The whole village is so extremely quiet that one tends to think one must be under observation even when one is not."

"It's a queer place," said Jeremy. "I don't remember its being as quiet as this on my other visits. I wonder what *that* building is?"

That building stood across the road from the village school and was built in the same kind of Victorian church architecture. On the door was a notice: *"No Young Persons admitted under the Age of Eighteen."*

"What can possibly go on in there?" said Jeremy, fascinated. "Do you suppose it's a night-club?" He tried the door. It was locked. "There's someone inside though," he said. "I can hear them."

"Come away," said Carreen, shocked. "They're probably having a Vergers' Congress."

"You're jealous because you wouldn't be allowed in." He tweaked his cousin's ear.

Deborah took no part in this exchange. She was thinking about the handwriting on Mrs Lewthwaite's door, and trying to remember where she had seen it before.

The afternoon had turned iron-dark, whisper-still. The houses of the village seemed huddled apprehensively among the leafless trees, like sheep waiting for snow.

"Evening comes early here," said Deborah, as they reached Jeremy's car. "I suppose it's because there's so little sky overhead." She looked at the sides of the valley climbing on either hand to slice off the horizon. "I think I should feel trapped if I lived down here."

"You'd probably never notice it after a couple of weeks," Jeremy said snubbingly. "Where *do* you live, Miss Lindsay? When you're at home, I mean?"

"In Canada. At least that's where I was born." What had been the intention behind the look he gave her?

"Are you planning to go back there soon?"

"When I've made my fortune," Deborah said lightly.

Mr Bridie waved as they passed his house and came hurrying out of the gate. Evidently he had just returned from somewhere, for his Rattletrap stood out in the road.

"So sorry I couldn't come up last night," he panted. "Called to the hospital—stayed with your uncle till the end —then I had one of my attacks—delighted to hear you're all keeping each other company up there. Deep regrets for your sad loss. He was a very old friend of mine—yes, well: that's how it goes. Meant to say I'll be delighted to come up now and help with the animals—know what rations John gave them and so forth, as I've been attending to them these last few weeks."

Evidently he knew all about Jeremy and Carreen.

"That's very kind of you," Jeremy said. "We'll run you up."

"Your aunt staying at the Trout?" Mr Bridie said as they drove up the zigzag track. "Never could stand Herondale House, could she? Well I remember how she walked out and went to live with her grandmother, when they were all children, the boys in their teens and she about nine years old. Never went back. Couldn't stand her brothers. 'Boys are horrible,' she used to say. Of course, her mother died when she was born, and I suppose it was rough for a little gel growing up in a family of males."

"I think *I* should have enjoyed it," Carreen said sedately. "I have always wanted a brother."

Mr Bridie chuckled.

"Different tastes, eh? You've a look of your aunt when she was young, nevertheless, decidedly a look of her." His eyes dwelt on Carreen briefly and Deborah noticed that beneath surface amiability their expression was cold, as if Carreen reminded him of something distantly unpleasant.

He went on, "Still, she was a clever gel, Marion. In her way she was equal to any of them. She'd tell one of the boys he didn't dare do something till human nature couldn't resist having a try. I'll never forget how Laurence broke his ankle climbing a cliff she'd said was impossible. She'd look at you with those dark eyes of hers—aye, she was always a good-looking gel, too—and say little, cutting, sarcastic things in that sweet way she has, till you were fair goaded into acting foolishly."

"She did something like that to me, once, about a gun," Jeremy said absently, twisting the car up a hairpin bend. "When I was a boy, staying with Uncle John. She had a house in the village then. Uncle John was out, away at a dog-show all day and she had me for lunch. Normally I'd never have dreamed of borrowing one of his guns without permission but Aunt Marion reminded me so many times that I mustn't—all the time implying that she couldn't trust me not to do something underhand—that in the end I did just that, out of pure cussedness. And then she whizzed along and told Uncle John about it the minute he came home. That fixed Aunt Marion in my mind, once and for all."

"Aye, old tricks work the best." Mr Bridie glanced sideways at Jeremy. "You'd be Laurence's boy, now? He was a grand lad. I was very grieved when I heard he'd been drowned. In a yachting accident, wasn't it? Went out when it was too rough? You'll have been at school then, maybe?"

"I was with my mother in Los Angeles," Jeremy said gruffly. "Father was staying with Aunt Marion at the time."

"Aye? Just so. Of course they all made up their little differences when they grew up. Marion will have been sorry she wasn't here in time to see John before his end; though they weren't on very friendly terms at the last, she always liked to know how he was doing. She'd contrive to get news of him one way or another."

Of course! thought Deborah. Mrs Morne had someone primed to write to her from Herondale. She remembered the letter in Mrs Morne's suite at the Arundel Hotel, on Herondale House paper that began Dear Mrs Morne. Not from John Gilmartin, obviously: a letter saying John Gilmartin was near his end?

Who could have written it?

When they reached the House they found the Daimler outside the front door and Gelert letting out fusillades of barks at the back. Willie Rienz strolled out of the door as Jeremy pulled up.

"I have just been depositing Carrie's luggage," he said pleasantly. "Had I known you were still in the village I could have saved myself a journey. Still, I am glad to have seen the House. A charming example of Georgian architecture, is it not?"

"How did you get in?" Jeremy said curtly.

"They keep a key at the Trout. I borrowed it, in case you had all gone off on some excursion. I will return it safely, never fear!" He beamed at them all and manoeuvred the Daimler expertly out of the small gravelled turnaround and over the hill.

"I'm not crazy about that fellow." Jeremy looked after the Daimler frowningly. "Why didn't he just dump Carreen's luggage in the porch?"

"Oh, come. He'd hardly steal your uncle's hunting trophies," Deborah mocked. "He was probably telling the truth—he wanted to see the House."

"You know him better than I do, of course, Miss Lindsay," he said coldly.

Deborah felt unreasonably irritated at this assumption but did not contradict it.

Mr Bridie took them round the livestock with careful instructions as to diet and management. Deborah and Carreen received tuition (with a good deal of hilarity) in the care of the ill-conditioned goat.

"I suppose your aunt will sell off all the stock?" Mr Bridie said. "If she does I'd be glad to acquire these Aylesburys. Nice birds. When's the Will to be read? This evening? Marion's all agog, no doubt. Everyone knows she's the chief beneficiary." His chuckle was not particularly friendly. "Now, is there anything else you need to know? The safe?— well, Proudshaw's got the combination, no doubt—but John never kept anything of value in it except a couple of ammonites and the bullet they carved out of him in Flanders. Pump? You'll not forget to pump once a day." He glanced up at the indicator—they were in the back yard. "Aye, if you pump this evening that should see you through," he told Jeremy. "It's wonderful how much more water is used by three young people than by one old hermit."

"Stay and have a cup of tea now," Jeremy offered, "then we'll run you back when we go down for the will-reading."

"I'll not say no."

Deborah put the kettle on while Carreen found cups and a teapot. Then Carreen took the jade-and-silver necklace out of its little box again, and held it up admiringly.

"It really is *very* pretty, Deborah; it was truly kind of you to think of giving it to me, when you didn't even know me. I shall have to find another sweater, though; I can't very well wear it with this red one."

"My lamb," said Deborah, "do me a favour, will you?"

"Of course. What is it?"

"Drop the necklace in the next unfrozen river you cross. I'd love to give you a present, anything you fancy—in fact I did intend to give you that—but it has—has acquired unfortunate associations for me. I'd simply hate to see you wearing it."

"Then of course I shouldn't dream of doing so." Carreen gave her a penetratingly sympathetic look, and Jeremy, who had come quietly to the back door while they talked,

81

startled them both by bursting into sudden song, in a pleasant tenor:

> *"I've never been one of the dashing bad girls,*
> *You can see that I never have strayed;*
> *For the wages of sin is a necklace of pearls,*
> *But the wages of virtue is jade!"*

He gave Deborah a grin, which she tried to quell with a stare of haughty non-comprehension, though she could feel her cheeks going pink. She was sure he guessed at some discreditable story attached to the necklace.

Jeremy lit the fire in the drawing-room and they had tea there. It was a pleasant room with a Chinese carpet and tinted engravings of flowers on the walls. Carreen wandered about studying the pictures while she munched biscuits. "What's a Jacob's Ladder, Mr Bridie?" she asked presently.

"It's a kind of blue Valerian, lassie, that grows in these parts. Elsewhere it's rare enough. Yes, indeed, this is a wonderful part of the country for wild flowers. And the one next it—Lady's-Slipper—is rarer still. One of the only specimens in England grows in this village."

"It's not very pretty," said Carreen, studying the pink-and-brown orchid.

"Just the same, botanists would come from a long way off to look at it."

"I'd like to see it. I suppose there's nothing showing at this time of year. When does it flower?"

"It flowers in the summer—but its whereabouts are kept a secret," Mr Bridie said, smiling his not altogether friendly smile.

"Oh, but—" Carreen began.

"—Mind, I'm not suggesting a little gel like you would dig up the root, or anything like that, my dear. But if I were to tell you, you might forget and tell someone else, and there are plenty of unscrupulous collectors about. Knowledge of that kind is best kept among the smallest number of people," Mr Bridie said primly.

"I suppose a few people in the village know about it?" Deborah said.

"Aye, no doubt. But they're a close, quiet lot, the York-shire dalesmen. They may know, but they'd never tell an outsider."

"Does Mrs Lewthwaite know, I wonder?" Deborah remarked, half idly. Mr Bridie darted a very sharp look at her. But he only answered in a vague tone,

"I really couldn't say . . ."

"The Lady's-Slipper—was that the wild flower connected with the Slipper Murder?" Deborah persisted.

"What was the Slipper Murder? Jeremy, you said something about that the other day," Carreen cried inquisitively. But Mr Bridie, looking as if he thought the subject an unsuitable one, was saying,

"And now, my dear young people, I should be thinking about getting back to my ain house. Aye, indeed, it's nearly dark."

Deborah, who had no intention of attending the will-reading, with which she was hardly concerned, said she would stay and keep an eye on the house. Carreen was inclined to remain behind too, but Jeremy told her she had better be present when the Will was read and meet Mr Proudshaw.

When they had all gone Deborah pottered about, washing the tea-things and thinking what a difference twenty-four hours' occupation made to the feel of the house; she was no longer rendered childishly apprehensive by the silence and the knowledge that empty fields and moors stretched away on all sides. When a cackling broke out among the poultry she thought robustly, "It's probably a rat," and took Gelert to investigate. Gelert sniffed and bayed, but no rat was to be seen.

Deborah decided that she might as well start the pump and generator while she was out. Having been put through a careful course of instruction by Mr Bridie, she now felt, as Carreen would have said, confident of success. In fact both engines started easily.

She waited a few minutes to switch the generator over to the diesel running fuel, and it was this that saved her life. As she walked towards the back door she heard a loud crack, and jumped back as something whizzed past her face to fall with a violent thud at her feet.

Stooping to pick it up, she found it to be the lead weight used as an indicator to mark the level of water in the tank. The rope had broken when it started to move up. So heavy was the weight that its fall had cracked the paving-stone by the back door right across.

Deborah picked it up with an effort. She felt a little giddy. If she—or Jeremy—or Carreen—had switched on and walked straight indoors—or had stood a moment, looking up to make sure the pump was working and the indicator rising correctly . . . She shut her eyes at the thought. Coiling the broken length of rope round the weight, she put it on a bench by the back door.

The water was starting to gush from the overflow as Jeremy and Carreen returned.

"Oh bother," said Carreen. "I wanted to exercise my newly-acquired knowledge and start the pump. Mind you let me do it tomorrow, cousin Jeremy."

Carreen looked white and excited; her eyes were extremely bright.

"Deborah, this piece of news is so amazing you will hardly credit it, but Jeremy and I are *heirs!* Isn't it delightful! Uncle John has left us this house jointly—till I am twenty-one, when either of us can sell his share to the other —and we inherit most of his money, too, of which there is a *tremendous* amount. Of course other people have legacies too—Mrs Lewthwaite has an annuity and her little house, and Mr Bridie had something, and Aunt Marion too, but nothing like so much, which seems a little hard on her, as apparently he had previously given her to understand that she would be getting it all. I must confess I feel sorry for her."

"Don't waste your pity, sweet coz," said Jeremy, who plainly was not doing so. "You should feel instrumental. Mr Proudshaw told me that it was your letter to Uncle John, explaining your difficulties about Marion and the playwriting, and asking his help, that decided him on changing his will. He wrote to you and me, inviting us up here as soon as we next reached England, and meanwhile summoned old Proudshaw and struck Marion out of a fortune the very next day. But of course he never expected to die so soon."

"Congratulations to you both," Deborah said carefully. "Carreen, I'm *very* glad for you—"

"But not for me, haughty Miss Lindsay?" Jeremy mocked. He too was unnaturally pale and bright-eyed. Deborah thought he looked as if he had been drinking.

"—because this means you can be independent both of your aunt and of playwriting till you want to begin again."

"Yes, isn't it exhilarating! Though of course in a way it was hardly necessary as Aunt Marion had turned out so unexpectedly prepared to consider my point of view with sympathy."

I wonder if she would now? Deborah thought involuntarily. Jeremy's sardonic brows, too, were questioning Aunt Marion's sincerity in this, and Deborah said hastily, "Honey, I hate to sound like a traditional nagging governess, but do you think perhaps you ought to go to bed? You look to me as if you'd be the better for a good rest. With all this excitement and the funeral tomorrow . . ."

"Yes," Carreen agreed, "that is an *excellent* idea. I need a period of calm reflection . . . Has anybody seen a couple of books on wild flowers? Hapgood's something-or-other Collection of British Wild Flowers, I think they were called —I was certain I had left them in the kitchen last night. Never mind, please don't trouble—I must have taken them upstairs after all."

After Carreen had gone her docile way Deborah showed Jeremy the lead pump-weight.

He said furiously, "Why didn't you wait to pump till I got back? I'd promised Carreen she could have a try. Now I suppose we'll run out of water; we shan't be able to tell where the level is. We'll have to let the stove out. You seem to have an infallible knack for making things go wrong—"

"For heaven's sake!" snapped Deborah. "Even if you are determined to lay everything that goes wrong at my door you must *somewhere* be accessible to reason! Can't you see the rope has been cut half-way through? Why should I want to do a thing like that? And if I did, would I then stand underneath?"

Jeremy, suddenly dead sober, examined the rope minutely.

"The rope hangs just outside the bathroom window," Deborah said. "Anyone could reach out and slice it with a razor-blade."

Their glances locked.

"Anyone who wanted Carreen out of the way," said Jeremy levelly. "Or me."

"Or you," she agreed.

"Or," suggested Jeremy, "anybody who wanted it to look as if one of us had a yen for murder."

Deborah slept badly that night. The cold was increasing. It pursued her through dreams of Mr Bridie smiling with a gun in his hand, standing in the doorway of his orchid-room, saying, "Knowledge like that is best kept among the smallest number of people," as he took deliberate aim . . . She woke shivering, and was glad to hurry down to the warm kitchen, where Jeremy was meditatively mixing pig-mash.

"Mr Gilmartin—" she said.

"Oh, do call me Jeremy, why not? Haven't we known each other long enough?" His eyebrows were two black circumflexes.

"All right, Jeremy . . . What will the arrangement be now? Are you going to live here—you and Carreen? Will Mrs Morne agree to that? Is she still Carreen's guardian? And—and where do I come in?"

"You stay here and teach Carreen, I suppose. Someone has to, after all, by law. The village school is hardly up to her mark, I imagine. Or do you mean, who is going to pay you?" Jeremy inquired acidly. "You'd better speak to Proudshaw about it; he's one of the Trustees of the Estate, who seem to have a say in Carreen's affairs till she is twenty-one. Marion never was Carreen's legal guardian; she had just quietly taken possession, nem. con, as the saying goes."

"But is Mrs Morne—"

"Somehow I doubt if we shall be seeing quite so much of Aunt Marion from now on," Jeremy observed with satisfaction. "Unless she tries to prove the Will was invalid. She seemed rather annoyed about the whole affair. Of course if you prefer her as an employer—if you don't like the hazards of life here—?"

"Certainly these aren't the circumstances I'd envisaged when I applied for the job." Deborah tried to sound brisk and businesslike. "Yesterday I'd made up my mind to tell Mrs Morne I couldn't go on with it—"

"Oh, well, in that case—" Jeremy mixed and sedulously inspected his pig-mash, "you must of course do exactly as you please. But don't leave us for a couple of days, will you, like a dear good girl? Carreen seems to be quite glad of your company, and with the funeral there's a good deal to be done . . . By the way, can you drive? If so, I'd be grateful if you could go down to Leigh and get us some pork pies or something like that; I gather we are expected to ask in the neighbours for a cold spread after the funeral. I hope Uncle John's doctor comes along so that I can buttonhole him; there are things I want to ask him. I missed him at the hospital."

"What are you doing this morning?"

"Aunt Marion wants to discuss financial affairs with me. Of course if you don't feel that doing my errands is any part of your duty, I'll do the shopping." He grinned rather sourly.

"Naturally I don't mind going," Deborah said.

Jeremy clanked out with his buckets, frowning, absorbed in the intricacies of his new life . . . She turned, with a feeling of deflation, to make the porridge for breakfast.

But as she set out blue bowls on a checked tablecloth, the very normality of her actions contrasted with the un-formulated doubts in her mind, and made these seem more substantial. At first they had not amounted to much: a silent village, a wandering fugitive whom no one seemed anxious to discuss, a missing pistol, a face at a window, a damp patch in a dead man's room—but now? The de-liberately half-cut rope could not be easily dismissed. Ought not the police to hear of it? And how would they account for it?

Suddenly she remembered that Willie Rienz had been alone in the house before they returned from the village yesterday. But then, for that matter, Mr Bridie or Jeremy could easily have slipped upstairs while they were all out dealing with the livestock—they had not all been together the whole time.

And where in this picture did Mrs Morne fit—Mrs Morne with her diligent correspondent in Herondale keeping her so abreast of village affairs that she was able to arrive in England just when her brother's illness reached a crisis? Mrs Morne had expected to inherit John Gilmartin's property—how much of a shock had it been when Jeremy turned up and scooped half the inheritance while the other half went to her own ward? And—a colder, more unnerving query—what was Jeremy's role in the business; where had he been the night before John Gilmartin died?

Jeremy's jacket dangled over the back of a chair where he had flung it when he put on a duffel-coat to feed the pigs; as Deborah moved the chair to set the table a shower of small change and a folded letter spilled out of the pocket. Absently she picked up the coins and put them back, noticing that the letter was written on Herondale House paper. In a crabbed, black, but clear handwriting she read the words, "My dear Jeremy, I do not know when you next expect to touch England, but I should like to see you again soon. Circumstances have decided me on making you my heir and I shall be glad if you can make it convenient to come up to Herondale as early as possible after this letter reaches you . . ."

Too late she heard the thump of gumboots and looked up to see Jeremy regarding her mockingly.

"Always on the qui vive," he said. "Were you ever a Girl Scout, Miss Lindsay?"

Deborah felt a furious blush cover her face and neck.

"I am extremely sorry," she said stiffly. "I hadn't the least intention of reading your private correspondence, I assure you. It was on the floor." Counter-attacking as the best means of defence, she went on, "Don't you think, by the way, that we should report that cut rope to the police?"

"Do you think it would be wise?" Jeremy said. His tone was rather odd.

"Certainly," she said flatly. "If you're not prepared to, I will."

"Well that's fine," Jeremy said gently, "because as a matter of fact I already have. I telephoned first thing this morning. Sergeant Herdman is coming up from Leigh police station to have a look at it this morning. So let's hope he can find some fingerprints on it. Satisfied?"

"Of course." She was baffled by his intonation; he went on, "I would also like to ask some questions about the damp area round the bed in my uncle's room. Someone left that window open for a long, long time, and I'd like to know whether Uncle John was in the bed at the time. Ice-cold rain blowing in on him isn't just the best thing for a sick man."

"Shall you ask the Sergeant about that?"

"I'd certainly like to ask *someone*," said Jeremy.

"Mrs Lewthwaite—" Deborah began. Then she said, "What did your uncle die of?"

"He had a bad heart condition," Jeremy said. "But what actually carried him off was acute congestion of the lungs. Pneumonia."

"When you were down at the hospital did you see the doctor who had attended him?"

"No; I told you. He wasn't available then, he was out on his rounds. But I hope to see him this afternoon."

Carreen came wandering in with her head bent over a book. She looked pale and heavy-eyed, as if she had slept badly.

Jeremy leaned over her shoulder, and read out, "Treason has done his worst; Nor steel, nor poison, Malice domestic, foreign levy, nothing Can touch him further."

"Really," Carreen said, "I can't imagine why anyone bothers to write any more plays. Shakespeare has done it all so much better."

"Perhaps in another twenty years they'll be calling you the Shakespeare of the twentieth century."

"Oh, I wouldn't want that," Carreen said earnestly.

"Why not?"

"I don't aspire to be the second Shakespeare. I want to be the first Carreen Gilmartin."

"You'll be the deceased Carreen Gilmartin if you don't get some breakfast into you this cold morning," Jeremy said, affectionately, rumpling her hair.

Deborah glanced at the window. The sky was yellowish-grey and ominous, but still the snow held off.

"I'll go to Leigh right away," Deborah said after breakfast, swishing detergent over the last of the blue bowls. "When it does snow, there's going to be plenty."

"I'll come too," Carreen said.

Jeremy shook his head at her. "Much better not," he advised. "You look as if you were starting a cold—and I'm afraid you really ought to put in an appearance at the funeral this afternoon. I should stay home and keep warm this morning. Deborah can manage the shopping, can't you, Deborah?"

"Easily," said Deborah.

"I'd rather go," Carreen said obstinately. Jeremy's brows met in a frown.

"I'm sure Aunt Marion would say—"

"But then you are not my aunt, darling cousin Jeremy," Carreen pointed out, giving him a cordial hug. She ran up the stairs for a coat and scarf, and hurried out after Deborah to Jeremy's aged car. He had left it in front of the house, as there was no shed empty; he now cranked up the reluctant engine for them. But he was still frowning as they left.

"Don't forget the double declutch!" he called after them as Deborah accelerated carefully up the slope and through the big gateway. The gravel was white with frost and the old tyres slipped and squeaked.

"You get a good view of the village from here," Deborah said as they topped the brow of the hill and were confronted by the breakneck drop beyond. "Or would if it weren't for the trees round it."

All that could be seen of Herondale was a few roofs set

in the dark group of trees against the fost-white planes of hill across the valley. It looked uninhabited enough. But the loud, cheerful chug of a tractor came up from the fields by the river almost directly below them, where a couple of men with a trailer were at work, carting winter feed. Load by load they were shovelling mangel-worzels out from a clump and carting them up a rutted track to a herd of bullocks in a more distant field.

"It's like a diagram of the strip-system," said Carreen. "Doesn't it look near? As if you could toss a pebble into that trailer. It's a lovely steep slope; it'll be marvellous tobogganing when the snow comes.—What's the matter?"

Deborah, very white, had her entire weight on the brake pedal.

"Good god," she gasped, "there's nothing here at all— these brakes are completely nonexistent. I've got my foot right down on the floor and still there's nothing—" She pumped at the loose pedal. There was absolutely no response.

Jeremy's car rolled serenely down the first slope of the zigzag track towards a left-hand bend while Deborah, still jabbing the pedal, tried unavailingly to get the stiff gear back into third.

Carreen's eyes were enormous. There was a trust in them that Deborah found terrifying.

"What shall we do?" Carreen said quietly.

"We've got to jump for it—now—before we get to the corner. Once over the edge there, we've had it. Open your door. I'll steer to the right—perhaps the car will slow down and stop when it runs on to the grass but we can't risk it. Are you ready? *Jump!*"

They both jumped clear. Carreen landed on the grass verge. Deborah fell sprawling on the stone-hard track, bruising her hip and grazing her arm. She pushed herself up and turned in time to see Jeremy's car describe a graceful swing to the right, pause on the first steep slope off the road, and then, all in slow motion it seemed, roll over on to its left-hand side and begin an accelerated bumping progress down the hill, crossing two more turns of the zigzag, and finally catapulting down the rocky slope into the river gully. A faint crash came up to them.

Carreen scrambled to her feet. "Good heavens," she said shakily, staring down. "What a lucky thing we— Are you all right, Deborah?"

"Yes," said Deborah, who felt sick. "But I'm afraid your cousin's car won't be much use again."

Already little figures were running out from the village towards the river, gesturing to each other, pointing up. The man with the tractor had made a sharp swing round and was jolting recklessly across the field, cutting black tracks in the frosty grass, losing part of his load at every hummock until somebody uncoupled the trailer.

"It was certainly not in your power to save the car," said Carreen, "if the brakes were as bad as that. Isn't it queer, though," she added slowly. "When Cousin Jeremy drove me up the day before yesterday I remember noticing that his brakes seemed unusually good for such an old car. And they were all right when we went down for the will-reading last night. I suppose they must have failed all of a sudden. I hope he won't be too upset."

"Yes," said Deborah, sharply remembering how Jeremy had urged Carreen to stay at home, how annoyed he had seemed when she flouted him. Was it real annoyance or had he—like Aunt Marion—counted on this reaction, deliberately urged her, by a dictatorially-phrased request, into contrary behaviour? He had started the engine—was there any reason to suppose he had not tested the brakes? If— if the accident was no accident, had it been aimed at herself or Carreen or both?

"I don't think I can face your cousin with this news just yet," Deborah said, carefully getting her voice under control. "He—he already thinks I am a sort of personal jinx on all machinery. We'd better go down and tell those people we're all right in case they think there's anyone in the river under the car."

"Your leg's bleeding—here, have my scarf to tie it up."

"It's all right, thanks, I've got a handkerchief."

Carreen helped her bandage the graze and they went rather unsteadily down the steep slope.

Mr Bridie was among the group by the river. He hurried to them with a shocked face.

"Are you unhurt, my dear young people? This is a most dreadful accident—I should have warned you to take extra care on that hill—I do hope Mr Gilmartin—?"

His bright eyes roved past them. The tractor had been backed up to the river-bank and two men were trying to get a rope under the wreck of the car, which was submerged in a rocky pool.

"Mr Gilmartin doesn't know about it yet," said Deborah. "I'm afraid he'll be horrified. The brakes failed completely at the top of the hill and we had to jump for it."

"Ah, these old cars, these old cars," Mr Bridie said, shaking his head. "Many of them are far from safe, especially in the hands of inexperienced young drivers."

"I'm not—" Deborah began protestingly, but he went on, "May I suggest that you come to my house for a hot drink which I am sure you need and then—I believe Mrs Whitelaw from the Trout plans to go shopping in Leigh this morning if that was your destination? I am sure she would be delighted to take you."

"Thank you," Deborah said, wondering how he had known about the shopping-trip, "but someone should tell Mr Gilmartin—"

"Sergeant Herdman is going up to see him this morning, I understand," Mr Bridie said blandly. "I am sure he can be entrusted with the sad news. He may also wish to inspect the vehicle."

"Just the same, I'll report the accident too," said Deborah firmly. "After all I was driving. There's a police station in Leigh, isn't there?"

The shopping excursion to Leigh had an air of unreality which Deborah made no attempt to dissipate. She bought provisions, ordered fuel, parried the hopeful curiosity of the shopkeepers, all with eighty per cent of her mind absented from the business. Carreen was equally silent, except once when she said, "Do you think I should buy something black to wear at the funeral? Jeremy said not, but what do you think? I've got a grey coat."

JOAN AIKEN

"Perhaps a black scarf," Deborah said. "Country people are very conservative. You don't want them to think you are not paying proper respect, particularly as you are a legatee. But it doesn't look as if there's a wide range of clothes to be bought in Leigh."

She wondered that Jeremy—who seemed, for a young man newly returned from roaming the world in cargo-ships, to have a remarkable grasp of the essentials of country-life —had not considered mourning wear necessary. But then, her mind added warily, had he perhaps reasons for believing Carreen would not be at the funeral?

While Carreen was buying the scarf, Deborah found the little police station and reported the fate of Jeremy's car, laying emphasis on the oddness of the fact that the brakes, which had been perfectly good the day before, should have failed so suddenly.

"Aye, it is a bit foonny," agreed the pink, shiny young constable who took down her statement—he and a buxom blonde policewoman seemed to be the only two people in the place and it was evident that Deborah had interrupted a rip-roaring flirtation—"but ye can never be joost one hundred per cent confident in these old ve-hicles. If the brake cylinder went, now— Any road, Sergeant Herdman is oop that way, he'll likely take a look at it. Thank you, miss. We'll let you know."

Deborah heard the giggles break out again as she left the room. She rejoined Carreen feeling thoroughly dissatisfied.

On the way back Mrs Whitelaw, who seemed to regain her natural cheerfulness when away from Herondale, gave free rein to a talent for gossip.

"I was that surprised when your auntie told me she'd be staying at least three weeks. Never could bear Herondale when she was a little lass; always planning to get away to London, she was. She sold that house her granny left her quick enough. I mind when she and Mr Bridie were engaged—"

"Aunt Marion and Mr *Bridie?*" said Carreen, fascinated. *"Truly,* Mrs Whitelaw?"

"Aye, luv; all set to wed, they were, when your auntie was twenty; but then she gave him the chuck and off to

94

London; folk said he hadn't enough money for her. You see when his dad died, that was the parson—Scottish he was, but a real nice body—it turned out that Mr Bridie wasn't as well-off as she'd expected . . . Leastways that's the story that went round."

If Mr Bridie had a vindictive nature, Deborah thought, it must have been delicately amusing for him when his ex-fiancée, eager for her legacy, came hot-foot back to Herondale only to be disappointed as he had been . . .

They passed a police car on the road back.

"Is there any news of the Slipper Killer?" impulse prompted Deborah to ask Mrs Whitelaw. "He came from this village, didn't he? Did you ever know him?"

"Eh, he was just a poor lad," Mrs Whitelaw said evasively. "There was a wild flower, you see, that he reckoned was his own special property, like, and he bashed a chap he caught digging it up. Folk reckoned the murder was more of an accident than anything else and that the Judge was too harsh with him; but really, you know, it's so long ago that I've forgotten the rights and wrongs of it."

Five years, Deborah thought. Hardly long enough to forget something that happened in your own village—not when you had such a clear memory for twenty-year-old gossip about engagements and legacies.

They were passing Blind Man's Crag. Carreen, looking up speculatively at the overhanging black cliff and shining pyramid of shale leading up to it, said, "Where did it happen? Cousin Jeremy told me a rare orchid used to grow up there. Was that the place?"

"Nay, luv, I couldn't say."

"The man might be hiding up there now," Carreen suggested. "Jeremy said there's a cave."

"Oh, the whole dale's honeycombed with caves. It's limestone country, you see—there's caves and potholes and underground rivers all over. When you go walking up on the fells you have to be main careful where you put your feet. What with the potholes and the bogs, it's best to stick to the tracks. Anyway," said Mrs Whitelaw, slowing up on the village-green, "like as not the poor creature's miles from here . . . Were you wanting to see your auntie now, luv, or shall I take you on up to the House?"

The first feathers of snow were beginning to drift down out of plum-grey, low-hung clouds as Mrs Whitelaw's station-wagon spun up the zigzag; Deborah thought the snow-flakes against the opposite hillsides looked like the advance guard of a swarm of locusts. The tractor still stood in the field below and Jeremy's car still lay under water, but no humans were to be seen; it appeared that the salvage must have presented unexpected difficulties or perhaps they had all gone off to lunch.

Mrs Whitelaw hurriedly refused their invitation to stay for a cup of coffee; she must, she said, get back for opening time.

Jeremy met them, quietly and whitely furious.

"I suppose it would be too much to expect that you'd have the common decency to let me know about the accident?" he said to Deborah. "I thought you'd both been killed, when Herdman came up and told me—and that I was to blame—"

"I'm terribly sorry about the car," Deborah said swiftly. "Please believe me that *no one* could have saved it. Both brakes went—"

"The car! My god, as if that mattered!" he exploded. "I've had Marion up here highstriking all over the place—Where was Carreen, why didn't I take better care, they were going to tell Proudshaw and have injunctions laid and Court Orders made out—I should have known we hadn't heard the last of Aunt Marion. I thought she'd behaved a bit too well over Carreen. I only hope she doesn't start an oration, now, at the funeral."

Suddenly and unexpectedly Carreen burst into tears.

"Oh, *p-poor* Uncle John," she wept. "He's only j-just dead and nobody thinks of him at all! Everyone's quarrelling and bickering as if—as if he had never been here. I *wish* he hadn't died."

Impulsively Deborah put an arm round the child's shaking shoulders, and flashed a look of warning over her head at Jeremy.

"Honey, you're all upset. That crash shook you up more

than you knew—it certainly did me. Why don't you lie down on your bed for a couple of hours and I'll bring you a hot drink—some soup or something."

Carreen nodded, gulping, and fled.

"Watch yourself in front of her, will you?" Deborah snapped at Jeremy. "I know she behaves like an adult, but she's only thirteen after all, and very highly strung— She's had a pretty gruelling three days—" She hesitated, feeling Jeremy's eyes intent on her, and added abruptly, "By the way, I made a full statement about the accident at Leigh Police Station. Did the policeman who came up manage to examine the car?"

"They've not been able to raise it yet," Jeremy said shortly. "It's jammed under a rock or something. They're going to go on trying this afternoon."

"Did you mention the pump-weight?"

Jeremy gave her his quick, expressionless glance. "Herdman said someone had cut the rope; thus confirming what we could see for ourselves. No fingerprints. He conducted a very thorough search all round the outbuildings and decided that someone had recently climbed over the garden wall. He also decided that it would be easy to get up on to the pigsty roof and reach the bathroom window from there. The only question that remains," said Jeremy, "is, who would have been likely to do this?"

Outside the kitchen window the snow had increased to a driving white flurry. A voice called, "Is anybody about?" and Willie Rienz came in, dusting white drifts off himself on to the paved granite floor.

"Your telephone is out of order, did you know?" he inquired. "I have reported it to the exchange. I have called to say I will come up this afternoon and drive you down to the funeral. I am so sorry to hear of the mishap to your car."

"Kind of you," said Jeremy remotely.

"It is nothing. We are in some sort neighbours after all." He beamed. "And the little Carrie—how is she? Not too shaken by the accident? I was looking out of my bedroom window at the Trout when it happened. I had a terrible five minutes, I can tell you!"

"We must all be grateful for Miss Lindsay's presence of mind," Jeremy said. The words were innocuous, but Deborah was disconcerted by the look the two men exchanged.

"I—I'm going to see if Carreen's all right," she said, and escaped.

"Give her my love," Willie called up the stairs.

By three o'clock, the time fixed for John Gilmartin's funeral, snow was falling heavily. The flakes came down and down out of the leaden sky as if they would never stop; already there was a thick, crunching layer of snow on the hard ground and lining the new grave.

The attempt to raise Jeremy's car had had to be abandoned for the time being.

Deborah had not intended to go to the funeral; she had felt it would seem intrusive, as she had never known the dead man and was no kin; but Carreen looked so white and pleading that in the end Deborah rode down with her in Willie's immense hired car. Jeremy had gone ahead with Mr Bridie to meet the small cortege coming up the valley from Cranton.

They joined Mrs Morne at the Trout. She was aloof and elegant in black and sables; Deborah reflected drily that the unknown correspondent in Herondale must have warned her some time since as to the probable need for funeral wear. Her dignity had not been impaired by the financial disappointment; Carreen received a ceremonial kiss, Deborah a gentle inclination of the head and a faint, surprised flicker at the correctness of her black wool coat. (In fact, Carreen had discovered her mother's trunkful of clothes in the attic of Herondale House and had pressed them on Deborah, using the black coat as a lever to persuade her to come and give moral support at the graveside; it fitted fairly well.)

No one was tempted to loiter after the brief, sad ceremony. Bitter cold drove them home. The fragile winter flowers in the wreaths were already stiff with snow. And although a group of friends and neighbours came up to the

House for cups of tea and the traditional cold ham and cake, they left mercifully soon in order to reach their homes before driving conditions became too bad. They were politely uncordial to Mrs Morne, and wary of Jeremy, to whom they said that they would have known him anywhere. Carreen, demure and well-behaved, they took to their hearts, finding her a touching and romantic figure. Deborah realised that probably no one in the village knew that this shy, straight-haired child was the author of four plays displaying a sardonic and tender insight into human nature at its most foolish. In fact Deborah herself found it hard to remember the fact, though she had long since fallen into the habit of treating Carreen completely as an adult and intellectual equal.

"I'm glad that's over," said Jeremy briefly, when the last of the mourners had left. "Poor old Uncle John . . . I wish I'd seen him again. Damn, I never did get hold of the doctor then."

"He wasn't here," Deborah said. "I asked Mrs Whitelaw. She said he'd been called out on an urgent maternity case."

Jeremy eyed her appraisingly. "You look as if you could do with a drink. Have you had one, or have you been too busy dealing out the plumcake?"

She shook her head and he picked up a decanter. "Here you are—funeral port. To keep out the cold."

It was sweet and potent and surprisingly cheering. Deborah felt dangerously relaxed, in the peace of the big library with its banked-up fire and empty crumb-strewn plates, Gelert snoring on the hearth-rug, the snow sifting down deeper and deeper outside the windows, the animals fed and bedded, the neighbours departed. The three of them remaining felt comfortably like a family unit, but that was an unsafe, subjective way of thinking, and must be guarded against. She knew she must be alert and vigilant. Mrs Morne had drifted up to her at one moment during the funeral tea, and murmured,

"My dear, I know you are not strictly in my employment any more but I *do hope* you are going to stay on with Carrie. I can see she has taken a huge fancy to you already and—well—it would ease my mind to know there was someone *sensible* like you with her. For instance this morning with the car—my dear girl we are so *indebted* to you. Need I say more? Jeremy—somehow I don't *entirely* trust Jeremy to remember Carreen's welfare at all times; she is only a child, and he is so much older and has lived a *rough-and-tumble* kind of life—and after all her interests do to some extent conflict with his, do they not?" Her dark eyes met Deborah's significantly and she added, "We must remember that if anything were to happen to Carrie, the whole property would be his."

"Surely you aren't suggesting—"

"I don't for one moment suggest that Jeremy isn't who he says he is," Mrs Morne agreed blandly. "All I *am* suggesting is that you need to keep a careful eye on Carrie. Because if anything—if anything *were* to happen, your *own* position would not be entirely straightforward—after all there was that little business of the necklace, remember? *I* know and *you* know that your integrity can't be called into question, but unfortunately there is nobody else to vouch for you, is there? People might feel entitled to doubts—they might believe that you could have been persuaded to help Jeremy—for a consideration, you know . . ."

Still smiling, she moved away among the comfortable red-faced farmers and their wives, leaving Deborah so blazing with anger that she was obliged to pull out a copy of Bewick's *British Birds* from the shelves and study it for a minute or two until she had command of herself.

It's not worth paying attention to a word the woman says, she thought. But just the same, the memory of this conversation lingered uncomfortably.

Carreen and Jeremy were dreamily and pleasurably making plans for their future.

"Shall you really learn to farm, Jeremy? Shan't you hate leaving the sea?"

"No, why? I only chose it as the completest possible contrast to life in Los Angeles. Matter of fact I've always wanted to farm. I used to come here and see Uncle John once or twice between trips, and I always thought that this would be the perfect place to settle, if one had a windfall.

Which reminds me, I must write to my mamma. She'll be surprised to find me setting up as a man of property— probaby be over here in a flash." His voice sounded momentarily bitter, but he added lightly, "What about you, little coz? You can hardly vegetate here for the rest of your life. You'll have to do something else besides write."

"I? Perhaps I'll go to college by and by. Could you coach me for that, Deborah?" she asked. Deborah nodded. "Then I'll travel, when I'm in my twenties, and come back here in betweentimes, perhaps. But I mustn't live in your pocket, Jeremy, after all. You might want to get married."

He burst out laughing.

"Not me! I shall be a recluse like Uncle John. Who should I pick? I don't suppose there's a wide selection in Herondale. But perhaps I ought to marry Deborah for the sake of the proprieties. What do you think?" His eyes met Deborah's derisively.

"I don't think much about marriage I'm afraid," she said shortly.

"Well, you should, an attractive girl like you.—Have you ever been engaged?"

"Yes. Once."

"Oh—ho," he said, eyeing her alertly. "And what happened? Did you frighten him to death, poor fellow?"

"I don't want to talk about it if you don't mind," said Deborah.

Carreen remarked, "I feel a bit tired and shivery, I'm going to bed."

Jeremy stretched and rose to his feet. "I'll stop the generator," he said. "Will you light some lamps and candles, Deborah? I'll have a look at the pigs, too, while I'm out. I don't know a lot about pigs, but a couple of them looked a bit odd this morning, I thought."

Deborah assembled and lit candles and lamps. She took one up to Carreen in the bathroom, then went downstairs again to stoke the boiler. A moment later the thump of the engine ceased and the lights all died, to be replaced by the feeble glimmer of the oil-lamps.

Suddenly there was a splash, a crash, and a scream from the bathroom upstairs. Deborah started hastily for the stairs with a candle. It blew out. Where had she left the torch? Ah—on the dresser. She grabbed it and ran up to the landing. The bathroom door was shut. She banged on it repeatedly, shouting, "What's the matter? It's me, Deborah!" There was no sound from inside.

Deborah rattled furiously at the latch. It was aged and frail and at last gave way. She burst in. Was that the window closing, or merely a curtain blowing in the draught? The floor was aswim with water and Carreen lay unconscious in the almost empty bath.

With feverish haste Deborah dragged the child out of the bath, laid her on a large towel, and started artificial respiration. In a minute or two Carreen coughed, brought up some water, and opened her eyes.

"What's the matter?" she said dazedly. "What are you trying to do?"

"Thank goodness you're all right. Here, wrap up in this."

Deborah half led, half carried Carreen along to her own room. "You'd better get into my bed, I put a hot-water bottle into it. Did you bang your head?"

"There's a lump," Carreen said, rubbing it with slow, puzzled fingers. "What happened? Did I slip? I remember the light blowing out. It was on the windowsill. I suppose there was a draught—"

"Never mind." Deborah administered aspirin, put on an extra blanket, glanced hastily round the room. "Don't bother about it. You'd better sleep in here with me tonight."

Her own window had bars—the room must at some time have been a nursery—so she felt fairly confident about leaving Carreen with the door locked. She took a lamp back to the bathroom and examined it. The window could have been forced—there was a scraped mark on the frame that might have been made by a blade, and scratches on the metal fastening, which was loose. Deborah shut the window as securely as possible and began methodically swabbing the floor to calm the trembling of her hands.

What could be easier than to go out, ostensibly to look at the pigs, turn out the lights, scale the outhouse roof, force the bathroom window, contrive a neat, accidental-seeming death by drowning, retreat the same way (all footprints to be covered by snow in five minutes) and then stroll in and say "What's happened to Carreen?"

"What's happened?" said Jeremy, putting his head round the door.

Deborah was so startled that she cried out, banged her knuckles on the tap, and swore.

"Nothing to speak of," she said briefly. "Carreen slipped and knocked herself. She's quite all right now." It was hard to meet his eyes but she managed it: a calm, creditable glance.

"Odd," said Jeremy, frowning. "Childish sort of thing to do. Did she tread on the soap? You're sure she's okay? Shall I have a look?"

"No, thanks. She's almost asleep." Deborah wrung out the cloth she had been using as a swab, picked up the lamp, and moved past him.

"If you're quite happy about her, come downstairs and have a drop more of my uncle's sustaining port," Jeremy offered. He put out his hand as if to lay it on her wrist. At that she did give him a quick, surprised glance, but his eyes were dark points of shadow, unreadable. Could he really think she was such a fool? Or was it a challenge? If so, she was not accepting it—but, oddly, a sort of contact flashed between them, a sort of acknowledgment—and then Deborah was saying, "No, I'm too sleepy, I'm turning in now. Thanks."

"Early to rise, and early to kip,
   Clears your complexion and reddens your lip,"

said Jeremy. He moved towards her indecisively, then checked himself, remarking, "I have an ungentlemanly impulse to kiss you, but something tells me that if I did, you would take the conventional way out and slap my face. How useful it is to have set rules of behaviour. One can be quite sure that kissing is not included in the terms of the relationship between you and me, Miss Lindsay!"

Deborah could think of no answer, and he did not seem to expect one. She walked to her own door, deliberately unlocked it, feeling his eyes on her, locked it again behind her and, standing immediately inside the door, said in a carefully pitched voice, "Carreen? Are you still awake? Move over, I'm coming in . . ."

She did not hear when Jeremy went downstairs.

Friday morning. Deborah slipped out of bed, leaving Carreen still asleep, looking defenceless and younger than her thirteen years with her mouth slightly open and dark hair tangled over her face.

During the night the snow had stopped falling but the sky, yellow-grey and threatening, promised more. A small, icy wind whisked white powdery eddies across the virgin surface of the stable-yard. Deborah pushed open her window with difficulty against a banked-up layer of snow on the outer sill, and looked down the valley. White, fading into grey, criss-crossed with the dark threads of drystone walls. Herondale, shrouded in its cobwebby trees, showed a few trails of smoke; otherwise there were no signs of life.

Cut off, Deborah thought dispassionately; people must get very odd here when, winter after winter, they are marooned with their neighbours, however uncongenial, for months at a time. No wonder small things—like wild birds, wild flowers—take on an obsessive, disproportionate importance. But then the people who live here appear normal enough—it is the outsiders—Jeremy, Mrs Morne, Willie Rienz with his grey face and bloodshot eyes—who seem unpredictable and frightening.

She dressed swiftly. Carreen had begged her to keep what she liked out of the trunkful of her mother's things and, finding a pair of warm waterproof ski-trousers among them, Deborah had gratefully accepted. Snug in these and a yellow sweater, she hesitated, wondering whether to re-lock the door behind her. Carreen opened her eyes and coughed.

"Early bird," she said drowsily.

"How are you feeling this morning, honey?"

"Sore throat. It hurts to speak," Carreen said with difficulty.

"Don't stir, then. I'll bring you up some porridge by and by."

"I don't think I could eat porridge," Carreen muttered apologetically.

Deborah laid a hand on the child's forehead and drew a quick breath of dismay. She went along to the bathroom, where there was a well-stocked medicine cupboard, found a thermometer, and, returning, put it in Carreen's mouth. Carreen smiled at her wryly, but Deborah motioned her not to speak.

During the night, choosing and discarding alternative courses of action, Deborah had made a plan. She would ring up Mr Proudshaw the lawyer who seemed, from what she had seen of him after the funeral, an intelligent and well-disposed if matter-of-fact little man, she would confide in him her fears for Carreen's safety and the story of the last few days at Herondale House, and would ask him to suggest some alternative domicile for Carreen and herself.

I don't trust any of them, Deborah thought, brushing her hair before the mirror and studying the result with unseeing eyes. They all stand to gain by Carreen's death. Mrs Morne has no further use for her if she won't write plays till she's grown up, and at present she presumably has control of the money Carreen has made, which she won't want to part with. And anyway the Gilmartin money is an even more tempting prize; with Carreen out of the way I bet Mrs Morne would find some means of making Jeremy go shares. She is certainly a past master at putting pressure.

Putting together what she had heard of Mrs Morne from Mr Bridie and Jeremy and Carreen, Deborah began wondering whether the whole of the shop-lifting incident at Port and Bellingham's could have been deliberately contrived, with the object of giving Mrs Morne a firm hold over her. It seemed a crazy idea, on the face of it, but otherwise what possible reason, motive could there have been? It occurred to her for the first time that there had been no real proof of the two men's identity as store detective and manager.

If you wanted a governess for a faintly shady set-up, to

teach a child who was being forced almost against her will into the role of juvenile prodigy, what better course than to pick a girl with no friends or relatives, a stranger in the country? There would have been time between her first and second interviews to check up on her story, to find that she was desperately hard up and in need of a job, knew nobody in England, had lost nearly all she possessed in the burglary. And then, if this girl was accused, before her prospective employer, of a humiliating petty crime, naturally she would be grateful and relieved to have the matter dealt with. But later on this obligation could be used as a handle to keep her amenable, to keep her from giving away the fact that Carreen Gilmartin's plays were not such unaided works of genius as was represented. And to make her—if necessary—an accomplice in putting moral pressure on an increasingly reluctant Carreen.

Deborah wondered then about Willie: what part did he really play in the menage? It took more than a strong will to coax dramatic masterpieces out of even such an intelligence as Carreen's; obviously someone else in the trio must have a streak of brilliance, and Deborah did not think it was Mrs Morne; shrewd businesswoman, excellent psychologist she might be, but she was obviously not creatively gifted. No, Willie was an enigma, with his beaming smile and his pouched, weary eyes. Perhaps Mrs Morne had some hold over him too?

Carreen coughed a little, painfully, and Deborah abandoned her thoughts and studied the thermometer. It registered 101°. Frowning anxiously, she hurried downstairs to make a hot drink. It was clear that she must get a doctor to the child and this presented a whole set of new difficulties: the impossibility of moving elsewhere with Carreen while she was ill, of summoning the doctor while the telephone was out of order—and would the doctor be able to get up to Herondale if the snow in the valley road was very bad?

Jeremy appeared briefly in the kitchen to gulp down some tea. He said that he was worried about the sick pigs and proposed to walk down to the village later on and ask Mr Bridie's advice.

"If you're going down, I'll come with you," Deborah said. "I don't like the look of Carreen, I think she may be coming down with flu. I'd like the doctor to see her as soon as possible."

"Do you think she ought to be left alone?" Jeremy asked dubiously. "I'll call the doctor for you if you like."

Deborah hesitated. She had been worrying over this point. She was indeed very reluctant to leave Carreen alone in the house even for so short a time as half an hour—but could she rely on Jeremy to transmit the right message?

As if reading her thoughts, he cocked a sardonic eye, and said, "It's all right, I haven't any accomplices at hand disguised as G.P.'s with little black bags all stuffed full of arsenic and strychnine. However if you don't feel—"

At this moment, to Deborah's relief, there was a tap on the back door. Mrs Lewthwaite came in, gumbooted and scarfed, to ask if they would like some help with the housework.

Deborah welcomed her thankfully. She found a comforting sense of normality in the presence of another woman about the house. Mrs Lewthwaite still looked tired, worried, and grief-stricken. She went silently about her work, plainly disinclined for chat, and Deborah respected this wish until Jeremy appeared saying that he would be ready to go in ten minutes; then she went in search of Mrs Lewthwaite and found her upstairs busy cleaning and airing John Gilmartin's room. She had a roaring fire in the grate, and the bedding hung round it on chairs and towel-horses.

She turned, startled, as Deborah, getting no reply to her first question, touched her on the shoulder.

"Eh, you scared me, miss! What was it you were wanting?"

"I'm so sorry. I wondered if you'd mind just keeping an eye on Carreen while we go down to the Trout to telephone the doctor. She's in bed with a chill and the phone's out of order."

Deborah tactfully turned her eyes away from the woman's deep, unbecoming flush, which slowly receded until she was pale as before.

"It's Dr Robson you want, miss; he lives at Stretton, only

a couple of miles down the valley. He'll be able to get up all right."

"Come and see Carreen," Deborah said. "I'm just taking her this hot-water bottle."

Mrs Lewthwaite, rather unwillingly it seemed, laid down her mop and followed. Deborah paused at her bedroom door; Carreen appeared to have gone back to sleep.

"I won't wake her," Deborah whispered.

Mrs Lewthwaite seemed to have something like a nervous aversion to approaching the bed. She stood a diffident twelve feet away and would step no closer—perhaps for fear of infection.

"Aye, she's got the family looks all right," she said briefly. "And now if you'll excuse me, miss, I've a kettle of water heating."

"You will keep an eye on her?" Deborah said, feeling oddly rebuffed by the woman's swift retreat. But it was true she had had a lot of sick-nursing to do of late. Mrs Lewthwaite turned from halfway down the stairs.

"Aye, I'll do that. She'll likely sleep till you get back."

Deborah fetched a coat from her room and ran down. Somebody had switched on the kitchen radio at top volume and an announcer's voice was booming from the library.

". . . here are the headlines again . . . Prime Minister's speech . . . Australia are 103 not out . . . More snow on the way for the northern half of the country . . . Police are still searching for 'Jock' Nash, the Slipper Killer, believed to be making for his home in Yorkshire . . ." The radio clicked off.

Mrs Lewthwaite came out of the kitchen with a bucket of steaming water. She passed Deborah unseeingly and went upstairs.

Deborah searched for Jeremy and found him in the warm, straw-smelling pigsty, leaning against the side of a pen with a worried frown.

"I wish I knew what was wrong with them," he said, staring down at the inmates. "They're good pigs. I'd hate them to die . . . after old John . . . He used to set store by his pigs."

The pigs certainly had an ailing appearance; they lay on

108

their sides in the straw with straight, limp tails and streaming noses.

"Do you think someone's been giving them chocolate?" Deborah suggested idly, fishing a couple of red-and-gold wrappers out of the litter. She could not help feeling that Carreen's illness was more important than that of any pig, however pedigreed, and her tone was ironic.

Jeremy, however, took the remark seriously enough. His eyes narrowed. "That's a damned funny thing," he said slowly. "How can those have got here? Sharp of you to spot them. I wonder . . ."

"Oh, I was only talking nonsense." Deborah tossed the crumpled paper away. "They were probably delivered with the straw, weeks ago. Are you ready to leave now? I'd like to ring the doctor and get back as soon as possible."

"Are you really anxious about Carreen?" Jeremy asked sharply.

"I'd like to know what the doctor thinks." Deborah kept her voice noncommittal.

The walk down through crisp, dry snow could have been exhilarating if Deborah had not been so worried. Jeremy, too, seemed to be nursing secret preoccupations, but he presently said,

"Do you know about nursing? Shall you be able to look after her or should we try to have her shifted to the hospital?"

"I doubt if she's as bad as that. In any case they probably wouldn't have a bed to spare. I know some things," Deborah said. "My father was a doctor."

"Was?"

Deborah nodded.

"He died in a motor crash, with my mother."

"Oh. So you're all alone in the world.—Was he a good doctor?"

"Yes he was!" Deborah snapped, stung by his cool, clinical, idle-seeming interrogation. "He was one of the best doctors I've ever come across! He went to endless pains to keep up with medical discoveries. And he *loved* his patients. He'd do anything to help them."

"All right, all right," Jeremy said, laughing. "I'm not decrying him. I'm glad he loved his patients. It's from him, then, that you get your burning interest in human nature?"

"From him—how do you mean?"

"Your interest in human nature," he repeated. "You study me, Miss Lindsay. You scrutinise me as if I were a lab specimen and you were waiting to see which fatal disease would throw out symptoms in me. Isn't that so?"

"Of course it isn't," Deborah said stiffly, but she felt herself blushing.

"Will it be alcoholism? Or drugs? Or just a nice, straightforward case of homicidal mania, starting with cousincide and ending like Lizzie Borden with a grand scene of wholesale mayhem, dicing up Aunt Marion, Mrs Lewthwaite, and Mr Bridie with a meat-axe?"

"You're talking nonsense. I can't think what you mean."

"Can't you? You have a pair of what I believe are known as speaking grey eyes, Deb—Miss Lindsay, and as far as I am concerned they speak volumes. They predict that I shall come to a bad end."

"Oh, stop it!" said Deborah wearily. All at once she felt beaten-down, miserable, and an exceedingly long way from home, not that she had a home. "Whatever you are getting at, I wish you wouldn't. I'm worried about Carreen, that's all. It's a big responsibility. And if she's going to be really ill in this isolated place, taking proper care of her is going to be no joke—"

"Okay, okay, relax. I'm sorry, duck." Much to her surprise, Jeremy gave her a couple of little pats on the shoulder. "It's a shame to tease you if you're really concerned about the kid. She'll be all right, though, I daresay. We Gilmartins are a pretty tough lot. And you can bet your boots that if it's anything over and above the common cold Aunt Marion will be up there posthaste, protecting her investment with the whole British Pharmacopeia at her back, in the hopes of binding Carreen with gratitude to write another half-dozen plays for her. So cheer up. And if she scolds you for not taking better care of Carreen I'll come into the box and swear that you never let her out of your sight night or day. It was the funeral that did it, I expect, funerals always start a new crop of illnesses."

"Darn it, I'm only trying to do my job," Deborah said, irritated by the irony in his penultimate remark. "And I don't know why I should have to defend myself to you."

"Full of prickles as a pin-cushion," he said gaily, but he threw her one of his wary, assessing looks. "Only trying to do your job—but what is your job, De—dear Miss Lindsay?"

Deborah did not answer him. She was staring up at the opposite hillside, where, above the tree-line, tiny black figures of men and dogs were toiling upwards. She said involuntarily,

"Oh—I wonder if those are the police searching for Nash. Are they police dogs?"

"Nash?"

"The Slipper Killer."

"Is his name Nash? I didn't know. . . ."

They passed in silence between the first houses of the village.

There were three or four police cars on the snow-covered green, and a general air of uneasy expectancy about the place.

"It looks as if the road to Leigh must be passable, anyway," said Deborah with relief. "I'll telephone from the Trout. Then I can tell your aunt about Carreen at the same time."

Mrs Morne was not yet down, so Deborah was able to put through her calls in privacy from the antique pay-box under the stairs among the stuffed fish in glass cases.

She was told that Dr Robson was away for a fortnight in Switzerland. "But," said the secretary. "Mr Gilmartin always had Dr Rumbold. He's up your way now, he was paying a couple of calls in Herondale this morning. Mr Croom and Mrs Galloway. They're not on the phone or I'd ring them for you, but everyone knows his car. You'll catch him at one or the other."

"Thanks," Deborah said, and rang off wondering why Mrs Lewthwaite had not given her the name of John Gilmartin's regular doctor; not that it mattered, but you would have expected her to.

When she rang Mr Proudshaw's office she learned with

dismay that he had contracted a bad sore throat at the funeral—Jeremy was right, it seemed—and was not expected back in the office for two or three days. She determined to write him a letter and obtained his private address. Now—ring the police about the possible assault on Carreen last night? But here was Mrs Morne coming downstairs, elegant and supple in lavender tweed. Deborah gently replaced the receiver.

"Hallo, my dear," Mrs Morne greeted her amiably. "Seizing the opportunity for a little winter-sporting? Willie is, too. Nothing would satisfy him but he must borrow a pair of skis in the village. Most people round here have skis or snowshoes; it must seem quite like home to you."

Home? Deborah thought of the gay little town where she had spent her childhood. She could not imagine anything more amazingly *unlike* it than this withdrawn, silent village sunk between the brooding fells.

"I expect there are some skis up at Herondale House," Mrs Morne went on. "Carreen's parents used to come here in the winter. Where is Carrie, by the way?"

"She's not very well," Deborah said. "A touch of grippe, I think. I'm looking out for a Dr Rumbold, he's supposed to be somewhere about the village."

Mrs Morne's eyes narrowed. "Carrie ill? That's unfortunate," she said sharply. "You're sure it's not something she's been eating?"

Jeremy strolled through the front door with his usual knack of arriving at a critical moment. "She's had nothing you'd disapprove of, I'm sure, Aunt Marion," he said amiably. "Did you find the doctor, Deborah?"

"No. He's supposed to be somewhere in the village. In fact I should be out looking for him now, so as not to miss him."

"I'll help you," Jeremy offered. "Bridie's going to come up and look at the pigs, but he has to water his precious orchids first. He says he'll run us up if we wait—it'll be just as quick as walking."

"Let me know what time you expect the doctor," Mrs Morne called after them. "I'd like to talk to him after he's seen her. You might ask him to call in here."

"Of course," Jeremy said courteously. "Where was the doctor going?" he asked Deborah as they crunched across the snowy green.

"Croom or Galloway—Mrs Whitelaw says one's by the church and the other's over the river, the first house along the Leigh road."

It was beginning to snow again; a criss-cross pattern of white flickered and dazzled between them and the houses on the opposite side of the green. The slopes of the fells were veiled. A little group of police were going purposefully from door to door. Others, with tracker dogs, were investigating shippens and outhouses.

Normally, Deborah thought, people would have been standing about and watching, either hostile or curious— but not in this village. Every door was shut, not a face showed at the windows.

"Do you know which family he came from?" she said.

"Who?"

"Nash, the Slipper Killer."

"No I don't," Jeremy said shortly. "I wasn't here when it happened. I don't remember any Nashes. Come on, we'd better hurry."

They crossed the humpbacked bridge over the rocky little river, which ran dark and full now, between white banks. Beyond lay the church, its ivy-hung tower crusted with snow, and the churchyard in which John Gilmartin's grave, wreaths and all, was lost under its white covering.

A hatchet-faced, shrew-eyed woman at Croom's farm told them the doctor had already been. "For what he's worth!" she snapped. "Same old mixture. Doesn't do my husband's cough a bit of good. They don't listen to more than a quarter of what you tell them. You might find him at Webb's, miss; he had a message to call there, her pains have started. That's the house by the post-office."

"We can try there on our way to Galloway's," Deborah said.

At Webb's a fat, anxious-looking woman, plainly the mother of the expectant Mrs Webb told them the doctor had called once and said he would be back later, but she did not know when. Leaving a message for him, they went on.

"There are two routes to Galloway's from here," Jeremy said, "as the village is in the shape of a double O. You'd better take one way and I'll take the other so as to be sure of not missing him. I'll meet you there."

He strode off into the whirl of snowflakes with a flip of his gloved hand.

Deborah hurried on, head down. Suddenly, for no reason that she could clearly define, she had begun to feel intensely anxious about Carreen, and was impatient to get back to Herondale House. With Mrs Lewthwaite there she should have no cause for worry—but still, she had this nagging urge to make haste, and almost ran up to the massive front porch of Galloway's farm.

There was no answer to her repeated banging. She tried the door. It was locked. Then she realised that it was probably only used for weddings and funerals. She went round to the back. Here a collie barked on a chain and a young girl whose prettiness was offset by extreme pallor and a look of strain said sympathetically, "What a shame, you just missed the doctor. If you'd been here five minutes sooner you'd have caught him. I believe he's gone to Webb's."

"Are you sure? I just came from there. Well, thanks," Deborah said, and started back, running and slipping in the powdery, deepening snow. She met two policemen with a dog and asked them if they had seen the doctor.

"Nay, luv," one of them said. "But we've just come out of yon barn; happen he could have passed while we were inside. There's chain-marks on t'road."

There were several sets of tracks; it was impossible to deduce anything from them.

"Is Sergeant Herdman in the village?" Deborah asked. "I want to see him badly. Something upsetting happened last night up at the House."

"He's oop the fell at present, miss."

Far above Deborah could hear the faint sound of baying.

"I'll tell him you want to see him. What was it happened, then?"

Deborah described the incident in the bathroom. Both men looked sceptical.

"Happen the little lass could ha' slipped and bashed

hersen," one of them suggested. "A body can easy enough do that, treading on t'soap, like. Still, we'll tell the sergeant about it for you, miss."

Deborah went on as quickly as she could in the soft, new snow, ignoring the picture-postcard charm of the small white-capped houses in their setting of tall trees. Hands in her pockets, head down, she was unaware till the last moment of a figure coming in her direction.

"Good morning!" a voice called gaily.

She looked up, startled, and for a moment failed to recognize Willie Rienz, who had exchanged his sober alpaca suit for mulberry-coloured ski pants and a brilliant parka. The effect was stunning. He carried a pair of skis and had just emerged from a side-lane leading in the general direction of Herondale House.

"Just trying the upper slopes!" he explained airily, noting with evident self-satisfaction Deborah's amazed glance at his costume. "There will be some excellent runs here presently. Ah, how it reminds me of my long-lost youth in the mountains! Do you ski, Miss Lindsay?" he added, turning to walk beside her. "Yes, I am sure you must, coming from Canada—you will be in your element here. We must go out together soon. But now, can I accompany you—are you off to market, or merely walking for pleasure in this charming village?"

"Neither," Deborah said. "I'm hunting for the doctor, who is supposed to be in the village—Carreen has a touch of grippe."

"Excellent devotion to duty—excellent. I applaud you. But," he said confidentially, "I should not take her ailments too seriously, if I were you. All the family are highly-strung, prone to these little psychosomatic touches—migraines, faintings, gastric complaints; a harsh word, a failure, an upset plan will bring them on and they are as easily cured. It is all self-importance, a wish to be the centre of attention—but you know this as well as I, Miss Lindsay—I am sure that you are a student of psychology. Between you and me, I imagine that Carreen is now feeling the after-effects of her little spurt of rebellion which fell so flat; that is her way. Not a doubt but she is now regretting this grand renunciation of a playwriting life—the praise, the excitement, the bright lights, they are not so lightly thrown aside when we are young, are they? In two days we shall find her secretively writing *Act I* in an old exercise book, mark my words—I have seen it all before! A talent like that cannot be turned on and off like a tap."

"Do you really think she feels like that?" Deborah said doubtfully. It seemed to her that Carreen's decision had more strength of purpose to it than he suggested.

"But certainly! And you will then be able to encourage her creatively, Miss Lindsay, like the wise girl I see you are. So much young genius there!—but it needs fostering, directing. I am happy that Carreen has already taken such a devotion to you—this can become a most profitable relationship. And you will turn to me for advice in any of her childish problems, will you not? Old Papa Willie has weathered so many of these small crises. Yes, yes, I can see we shall make a famous partnership, we three! Soon the plays will be flowing out again."

"I haven't the least intention of encouraging her to write unless she really can't resist the urge to," Deborah said decisively. "I think that would be extremely wrong. After all, she has no need to, financially; she's well provided for now."

"Of *course,* of *course,* darling Miss Lindsay! But she *will* feel the need to create, you will see. Can you imagine William Shakespeare not feeling the urge to write *Antony and Cleopatra?* Carreen is *driven*—she is driven by that unbalanced, manic compulsion that drives the whole family. —Besides," he added, "she may not be so well provided for. Marion is disputing the Will, naturally—and Marion has good lawyers."

"On what grounds can she dispute it?"

"Oh, of course, on the grounds that John altered his will in a state of temporary mental derangement. He, too— really, it is as well you should know all this, Miss Lindsay. There is great mental instability in the family. That was why John never married, why Marion's husband left her, because of her queer moods, her ups-and-downs, her migraines. As for young Jeremy, the taint has come out in him strongly, I fear. His rages when he was a boy, so I have heard, were quite ungovernable; he half-killed another child for touching his bird's-egg collection, and there was a *most* discreditable episode with a schoolmistress which had to be hushed up. Yes, the sooner Master Jeremy goes back to his rovings on the high seas, the better everyone will be pleased, I imagine."

"He *said* he was going to stay and farm——"

Willie shook his head incredulously. "That young man never keeps to a plan for more than a month or two. We shall not see him for long."

Deborah stood still. A curiously hollow feeling had taken possession of her. Before, at the Arundel Hotel, she had found Willie steadying and reassuring. Now, everything he said tended to trouble and disturb. But she tried to shake herself free from his influence; this was not a moment for introspection.

"I'm going to call at this house, Mr Rienz," she said—they had reached the Webbs' again and she noticed hopefully that a car stood outside—"the doctor may have come back here. Thank you for your company."

"A moment, my dear." He laid a hand on her arm. "And please call me Willie! I know that we are going to be good friends, there is no need for formality! Remember what I háve said: if at any time you need advice, old Willie is ready and waiting. We two could work together very well, *very* well—do not forget."

Deborah was greatly disconcerted by the look in his pale eyes, still more by the feel of his hand on her arm and the proximity of his body. It was like, she thought confusedly, standing close to some big, humming piece of machinery; it was so controlled that you did not realise until you approached it closely the formidable amount of heat and power that it generated.

"Oh—thank you," she said. "But I'm not going to do anything that isn't in Carreen's own interests," and she stepped away from him rather too fast for courtesy and hurried up to the Webbs' door. After knocking she turned to see Willie still regarding her intently before he turned and, with a flourish of his hand, walked away into the falling snow.

Mrs Webb's mother answered her knock and looked conscience-stricken. "Oh, miss, it went clean out of my head! The doctor's been and gone again up to Blighs'—yoong Bligh joost brought word his Dad had a nasty fall and they're afeered he's broke his arm. I was that put about wi' my poor Peg—eh, she's in a reet bad way wi' her first—I never laid mind to your little lass."

"Oh my goodness," Deborah said, while the woman repeated her apologies—but did she really mean them, had she really forgotten? She seemed distracted and nervous, looked everywhere but at Deborah. "Whose is the car, then? I thought it must be the doctor's."

"Nay, it's the midwife, luv—thank the lord she's got here at last."

"Where is the Blighs' house—will the doctor be coming back this way?"

"Likely he won't," the woman said guiltily. "Happen he'll go over t'fell and round to Cranton by t'other road. He'll be back agen tonight or tomorrow, he said."

"How far is it to Blighs'?"

"Matter o' two mile oop valley."

"I've had it then," said Deborah. "I'll never catch him now," and she turned to go back towards the centre of the village. Mrs Webb's mother had hardly waited to listen, the door was already closing on her plump, worried face.

Deborah hurried, this time with the snow driving behind her, sliding between her scarf and the back of her neck. Hopeless to hunt any longer for the doctor, he would get her message at the surgery and no doubt he would call next time he came up the valley to the Webbs'. Now she had best get back to the House as soon as possible.

While she struggled along the narrow, rutted road her mind ranged perturbedly over the hints—you could hardly call it information—that Willie had so artlessly let fall. Resolve how she might to take no notice of his innuendoes, Deborah yet could not help uneasily speculating about the family unbalance he had alluded to. What had been the matter with old John? Was it really a heart condition? What was the tale about Jeremy and the schoolmistress? How had Willie come to know about it? And what was that earlier remark—something that had startled and mystified Deborah at the time but now slipped her memory, overlaid as it was by worry about Carreen. No, it had gone, but it would come back—probably to trouble her in wakeful stretches of the night.

Jeremy had not yet returned to the Trout when she got back there, but Deborah told Mrs Morne about her vain pursuit of the doctor.

"Would you like to come and spend the day up at the House so as to be sure and see him when he does come?"

"Sweet of you to offer but I can't do that," Mrs Morne said coolly. "For one thing Willie's just gone off with the car, and for another I'm expecting a telephone call from my lawyer in London. No, you ask the doctor to drop in here when he's been, then I can ask him what's the matter with the child. You'd better be hurrying back to her now, hadn't you?" Mrs Morne's tone was delicately critical.

"Mrs Lewthwaite's with her," Deborah said quickly. "I'm looking for Jeremy—Mr Bridie's supposed to be driving us both back. Have you seen him?"

"No, my dear," Mrs Morne said absently. "He hasn't been in here . . . Mrs *Lewthwaite,* did you say? I shouldn't have thought, in the circumstances, that she'd be quite the best person . . ."

Looking out of the parlour window Deborah saw Jeremy hurry across the trampled white in front of the Trout. The hood of his duffel-coat was pulled forward over his face but she recognised his stride. He looked up and caught sight of her with Mrs Morne. His black eyes narrowed and he made an impatient gesture.

"There's Jeremy, I must go," Deborah said hurriedly, and ran out.

"Here you are," Jeremy greeted her. "I've been hunting for you all round the village. Bridie's waiting for us "

"I just missed the doctor—he'd already left and gone to a farm called Blighs'."

"You *still* haven't caught him?"

He turned to stare at her and she thought there was an unfriendly look in his black eyes.

"No," Deborah said crossly. "Mrs Webb saw him again

but forgot to mention that we wanted to get hold of him."

"Oh well, I suppose we'd better abandon the attempt for now. You left a message at the surgery, did you?"

"Of course I did," Deborah snapped. "I'm not absolutely dumb."

They finished the rest of the short distance to Mr Bridie's house in silence, walking slightly apart.

Mr Bridie, it turned out, had just gone to the post-office in his car; the housekeeper let them in saying he would be back in five minutes and would they care to sit down? She showed them into his chintzy little front room where Deborah had been once before. Deborah sat reluctantly, then stood up again.

"I think I'll start walking up the hill," she said. "Just in case he's held up and doesn't get back for a bit. I hate leaving Carreen for so long."

"Oh, rubbish, she's all right with Mrs Lewthwaite. There's no point in tiring yourself—you won't get there any faster."

But Jeremy himself seemed restless; he fidgeted about the room, picking things up and putting them down, then wandered to the window and stood looking out with his hands in his pockets.

"The police seem to have drawn a blank," he observed. "They are going on up the valley. I must say my sympathies are all with the hunted on occasions like this."

"Oh, so are mine—" Deborah said impulsively. Her words were cut short by the entry of Mr Bridie who came through the house from the back, rubbing his hands briskly.

"So sorry to keep you waiting, but I daresay you could do with the warm-up," he greeted them. His strange eyes were brighter, his grey hair more flyaway than ever, and he had his usual rather disconcerting air of amusement over some hilarious private joke. "I'll just fetch Rattletrap to the front —Anne! Give the young lady and gentleman some sherry!" Without waiting for an answer he disappeared again. The housekeeper came in and poured pale, straw-coloured sherry out of an elaborately cut decanter.

The sherry was icy cold and so dry it made Deborah's hair stand on end; she would have liked to leave it but was afraid of hurting Mr Bridie's feelings.

Replacing her empty glass on top of the open bureau where the tray and decanter stood, she caught sight of a newspaper cutting among other papers on the desk. *Society Witness in Court Case* was the headline, and the face in the picture above it was tantalisingly familiar. Who——? Where——? She was still sorting fruitlessly through the last three days' chaotic memories when Mr. Bridie chugged past the front window in his Rattletrap and gave them a roguish wave.

"That's for us," Jeremy said, and strode to the front door. Deborah followed, glancing towards the little conservatory where Mr Bridie kept his exotic flowers—but somebody inside slammed the half-open door as she passed it.

"Get the doctor all right, did you?" Mr Bridie said, and Deborah explained the failure of her mission.

"Blighs'? Oh, but that's no distance," Mr Bridie said, holding the car door for her. "I can buzz you up there right away and we'll catch him before he goes on. Yes indeed, that's what we'll do, glad to be of use." And he shot the car along to the foot of Herondale Hill, described what felt like a very dangerous skidding turn at the foot, and cut into a small back lane that joined the main valley road opposite the Webb house.

"Oh, I didn't mean you to— Really, I think it would be better if we went straight home now. It's terribly kind of you but I feel I've left Carreen for such a long time already," Deborah protested.

"No, no, quite all right, m'dear, we must all help each other, get into the habit in these little isolated communities," Mr Bridie said gaily, continuing to drive very fast but turning to look at Deborah in the back, so that his car did a horrifying slither with the front wheels turned at right angles, so far as she could judge.

"But the doctor may have left Blighs' already and then we shall have wasted more time."

"I shall be surprised if he has. They brew a first-class sloe gin at Blighs', absolutely first-class, ha ha! Old Rumbold doesn't often leave under half an hour when he calls there."

"Really it's more sensible to catch him now if we can, isn't it," Jeremy said to Deborah. "You're not being very consistent about it, are you? I thought you were so anxious to get a doctor to her."

"*You* said yourself that we'd better abandon the attempt. *You're* being even less consistent."

"Do not let yourselves be harried by anxiety, my dear young people," said Mr Bridie, who for some reason seemed extremely amused by this exchange. "In any case part, at least, of your doubts may be set at rest, for there across the valley I see Rumbold's car outside the Bligh house. Red is a deplorably vulgar hue, in my opinion, but useful, undoubtedly useful, as a distinctive feature."

"Oh, I do hope he doesn't suddenly come out and drive off!" Deborah exclaimed, clasping her hands in anxiety; she felt that Mr Bridie's Rattletrap had small chance of overtaking the sleek red convertible.

"I will warn him," Mr Bridie said, and squeezed out several prolonged blasts on his ancient hooter, before turning and carefully negotiating a small bridge. The road crossed the valley, much narrower here, and passed the substantial Bligh farm before climbing at a crazy gradient up on to the fell. The river seemed to have vanished; under the bridge there was nothing but a snow-lined indentation.

"Rivers come and go in this part of the country," Mr Bridie explained instructively, noting the direction of Deborah's glance. "They dry up—or rather, they sink into the ground, run into a cave, and pop up somewhere else. Old Bligh was fit to be tied when his bit of river went underground; the Water Board dropped vegetable dye into the water up above and it came out below Cranton; he's been trying to sue the Cranton Council for wrongful misappropriation ever since, heh, heh. Now, here we are, and there is Dr Rumbold; dear me, he seems to be taking poor old Bligh away. This complicates matters."

The doctor, duffel-coated and grey-haired, could be seen carefully assisting an elderly man with his arm in a sling into the front seat of the red car.

"Hello, there, Rumbold! Don't go for a moment, we've another patient for ye," Mr Bridie called, coasting to a halt a few inches from a stone gatepost. Deborah tumbled out of the car, with Jeremy behind her.

"Can't stop, must get Tom here to hospital," the doctor called back authoritatively. "Have to put a cast on him as soon as poss——" His jaw dropped and his eyes widened, looking past Deborah.

"Eh, I'm sorry to hear you've hurt your arm, Tom," Mr Bridie said concernedly. "Rumbold, this is young Gilmartin, Laurence's boy, you know, and Miss Lindsay, who's looking after little Carreen—Miss Lindsay, you'd better do your own explaining, you know the symptoms."

Deborah hurriedly described Carreen's condition while the doctor went on with his task of expertly packing his patient into the car with coats and a pillow.

"Temperature, has she?" he said. "Sore throat? May not be anything too bad. Well, I'll get along to see her as soon as I can, after we've plastered up Tom, here—in the meantime, keep her warm and give her plenty of fluid. Maggie!" he bawled, turning towards the house, "bring's another cushion, can you? Right, Tom, I'll try not to jolt you more than I can help; sorry to do it this way, but if we waited for the ambulance we might wait till Spring."

"Dr Rumbold," Jeremy said.

"Yes?"

All the doctor's words and actions were so brisk and sharp that each remark came out as a snap. Deborah decided that he was not really unfriendly or hostile; it was just his natural manner.

"You looked after my uncle when he died?"

"Yes, I did," Dr Rumbold said, glancing at his watch. "What the devil is Maggie doing now? Maggie! Hurry up! I'm supposed to have a clinic in twenty minutes."

"I'd be glad if I could come and talk to you about his death some time, or perhaps we can have a word together when you come to see my cousin?"

"Yes; well, all right, though there's nothing to discuss, you know. Perfectly straightforward case, might have happened any time these last ten years. I'll look in this evening or to-morrow; can't say when."

Deborah moved back towards Mr Bridie's car, wondering in what respect Dr Rumbold reminded her of the fat woman she had talked to, the expectant Mrs Webb's mother; what was the point of similarity? Rather reluctantly, Jeremy turned to follow her, as the doctor was taking no further notice of him.

"Ah, there you are, Maggie! What the devil have you been doing, digging out the best goosefeather bed?"

"Just putting up a flask of summat 'ot, Doctor, for you to take along," the farmer's wife said placatingly, hurrying towards the car with a thermos and a folded quilt. Then she gasped, turning chalk-white; the flask she carried thudded into the snow as her hand flew to her mouth. "Susan!" she gasped. "Heart alive, has Susan——" Her legs seemed to collapse under her and she fell in a crumpled heap.

"Tchk, tchk, tchk," the doctor said crossly. "Always such a one to faint, your wife, Tom. The least little thing and over she goes. No, don't you get out——" as the agitated farmer, exclaiming inarticulately, tried to open the door—"you stay where you are, we'll manage her. It's just the cold and the upset. Oops, lass! Here, you, what'syourname, Gilmartin, can you help me carry her in?"

She was a slight, thin woman; the doctor and Jeremy between them had no difficulty in carrying her into the house. Meanwhile a young girl ran out, picked up the fallen flask and the quilt, and reassured the elderly man.

"Don't tha worry about her, Dad, she'll soon be all reet. I'll make her a cup of tea; you know how she is wi' these turns."

"Keep her quiet for half an hour, Rose, and she'll do," the doctor called, reappearing. Jeremy followed him silently and got into Mr Bridie's car, while the young girl, Rose, cast a curious glance at him.

"Right? Then we'd better be off," Mr Bridie said, and manoeuvred his car round and back the way they had come. "Poor old Maggie Bligh," he said, laughing, as they recrossed the waterless bridge. "Faints in church, faints at whist drives, faints at cricket matches—somebody said once, the only place she wouldn't faint would be at her own funeral. She's certainly fainted at everybody else's. I don't know how the daughter will ever be able to marry and leave home."

"She seemed to faint at the sight of Jeremy," Deborah remarked involuntarily.

"Eh, no, it was just upset at Tom's accident, I expect," Mr Bridie said, his breezy manner somewhat belied by the crease between his brows. Jeremy remarked acidly,

"Quite a few people have told me they didn't particularly care for my appearance, but this is the first time I've heard it suggested that someone would *faint* at the sight of my face; hardly a flattering idea."

"Something like the Gorgon's Head, eh?" Mr Bridie suggested cheerfully, and began all at once to tell a long, gay, pointless story about an artist who had repainted the Trout Inn sign one summer and an old lady who saw the new sign propped up against a wall drying and mistook it for her intoxicated husband. "Poor old soul, she was teased about it from one end of the valley to the other for months after; she hardly dared to look you in the eye in case you began."

Like plenty of other people, hereabouts, Deborah thought. Like Mrs Webb's mother. Like the doctor. That was the point of similarity. He looked in his bag, or at the man in the car all the time he talked; she looked at the floor. So does Mrs Lewthwaite. What's the matter with the people in this village?

She glanced about her for other inhabitants as they drove back, but saw none, though they met a couple more clumps of police along the road, with their dogs. Mercy, Deborah thought, what weather in which to have to hunt down a murderer, and what weather in which to be skulking and hiding and running for one's life. She felt sympathy for the wretched Nash, but her anxiety for Carreen by now overbore all other considerations. As Mr Bridie swished his Rattletrap round the difficult bend at the foot of Herondale Hill and began a cautious ascent of the slope she found herself mentally pushing the car every foot of the way, willing it not to stall and waste more time. Yet, curiously, now, just when her mind seemed labouring under extreme strain, a little porthole of memory opened and she thought of the press-cutting she had seen on Mr Bridie's desk. She remembered the man's face in the picture. It was—she was beginning to get warmer now, in a moment she would have the clue—it was associated in her mind with some recent unpleasant occurrence.

"And here we are, safe in wind and limb," Mr Bridie said,

triumphantly bringing Rattletrap to a slippery halt in front of Herondale House. "Now, which are these ailing pigs? To be candid with you, I suspect they've nothing much the matter with them, but with pigs you're better safe than sorry and the vet lives a devil of a way off, t'other side of Cranton . . ."

Of course! thought Deborah, so astonished by her discovery that she jumped out of the car without thanking Mr Bridie and went automatically indoors; of course the man in the picture was the store detective at Port and Bellingham's, the man who "saw" me steal the jade-and-silver necklace. It wasn't a good picture, but I'd be almost sure. If only I could get another look at the cutting to see what it was about!

Still pondering the implications of this discovery, she walked through to the kitchen, searching for Mrs Lewthwaite. All the rooms were clean, tidy, and warm, but Mrs Lewthwaite was nowhere to be seen. Upstairs, perhaps, sitting with Carreen? Deborah ran up, calling, "Is everything all right, Mrs Lewthwaite? Sorry we were such a long time—" and then came to a halt, dumbfounded, on the threshold of her room. The bed was neatly made and there was no sign of Carreen. The room next door was similarly neat and empty.

"Carreen!" Deborah called. "Where are you?"

Increasingly startled and uneasy, she looked swiftly into every room on the first floor—noticing that all the furniture in the big front room was now dried and set in order—then ran downstairs again. The house was empty. Mrs Lewthwaite and Carreen were nowhere to be seen.

Deborah stood still for a moment, really at a loss what to do. The neat, warm emptiness of the house mocked her. She tried to think of plausible reasons for Carreen's absence: the child had felt better, had decided to go for a walk; Willie had called with the Daimler to take her sledging; Mrs Lewthwaite had been summoned urgently to the bedside of a sick relative, had not liked to leave Carreen, and had taken her along too. With a high temperature? Each suggestion was more improbable than the last.

Perhaps Mrs Morne, growing uneasy about Carreen, had decided to fetch her down to the Trout? That was a more feasible idea, but they had passed the Trout on their way back from Blighs', and somebody, surely, would have been on the look-out to intercept and warn them.

It was worth inquiring, though, and Deborah moved to the phone, only to find, with a sinking heart, that it was still out of order.

She heard voices and the stamp of gumboots by the back door. Jeremy and Mr Bridie came along the little passage, shaking off snow.

"Deborah, is there any coffee among my uncle's stores? A cup now would be a life-saver," Jeremy called.

"If you ask me," Mr Bridie was saying, "all those pigs are suffering from is a nasty chill. I'll lend you my infra-red lamp—"

"But how could they have got a chill? They're snug enough in that pen—"

Deborah could have laughed at the idea of an infra-red lamp for pigs if she hadn't been so worried. Forgetting her reservations about Jeremy, she ran to him and clutched his arm.

"Jeremy, Carreen's missing! Have you any idea where she could be? She's not in her bedroom—she isn't anywhere in the house! And neither is Mrs Lewthwaite!"

"You can't mean—" Jeremy was startled. "She *couldn't* have been such a damned litle fool as to get up and go out in this?"

Deborah turned to the window. The snow was really racing past, now, in long, swirling veils of white which for moments together cut off the view of the buildings across the stableyard.

"Dear me," Mr Bridie said perturbedly. "Are you certain that you have thoroughly searched the house, Miss Lindsay? And called? Let us all shout together."

They all shouted: "Carreen! Carreen! Where are you?" There was no reply.

"What about the outhouses? Or the stables? Perhaps some childish prank of hide-and-seek?"

"Hardly, Mr Bridie. She's—she's not that kind of child. Reading *Hamlet* in the library is more her line. But anyway she was *ill*—she had a fever—all she wanted to do was stay in bed and sleep."

Deborah looked distressfully from one man to the other.

"I bet Aunt Marion has come up and whisked her off." Jeremy was beginning to look angry. "It would be just like her to do that, regardless of whether Carreen wanted to, or was fit to be moved—" He started towards the telephone.

"The phone's still out of order," Deborah said. "And anyway, don't you see, if Mrs Morne had done that, someone would have told us about it as we came by. Or at least they'd have left a note here. Don't you think we ought to tell the police? I know it sounds crazy, but I'm so worried—" Her voice trembled, and she stopped miserably, biting her lip.

"Don't worry, ducky, we'll find her all right. And we *will* tell the police, if we can't pin her down in half an hour," Jeremy said.

Deborah looked at him gratefully, part of her mind noting with vague surprise that this was almost the first time he had said anything to her sounding sincerely friendly.

Mr Bridie blinked. "Is not this rather precipitate?" he suggested. "Are you certain she has not somewhere left a note for you? Perhaps she decided to go home with Mrs Lewthwaite for some reason."

"She couldn't have been so *crazy*," Deborah said impatiently. "Mrs Lewthwaite walked up here—surely she wouldn't have expected Carreen to walk down to the village through this kind of weather?"

"Ah, well, you know, country people," Mr Bridie said vaguely. "They have spartan ideas about health; children walk miles to school, that sort of thing. But I do recommend you to look for a note. I am sure you will find that she has left some message."

They hunted in all the likely places but no note was to be found. Another and more thorough search of the house and outbuildings was equally fruitless and only confirmed that Carreen was gone. Her small overnight-case was missing too.

"It begins to look like a flit," said Mr Bridie sceptically. "Did she not run away from her aunt in London?"

"How did you know that?" snapped Jeremy.

"Mrs Whitelaw told me; she heard them talking about it at

the Trout." Mr Bridie smiled at him placidly. "Maybe she's done it again; feverish, you know, light-headed; afraid, maybe, her auntie's going to put on more pressure, and so she's up and off. Isn't that a possible theory? She seems an independent young lady."

"No, I'm sure it isn't," said Deborah almost weeping. "Carreen's such an adult, considerate, *gentle* child; even in London, when she had been placed in an impossible position by her aunt, she left a note explaining what she was doing and telling them not to worry. I'm certain she would have done as much for us. She wouldn't have left us guessing. After all she knew we—we had nothing but goodwill for her."

"Did she?" said Jeremy. He gave her his mocking, disturbing look. "Did we?"

"Well, I'm going to the Trout to ring the police." Deborah started towards the door and Mr Bridie hurried after her.

"I will run you down of course," he said. "The chances are that the police are still in the vicinity and naturally, in—in the circumstances I imagine they will be very ready to help you."

The thought—which Deborah had been pushing to the back of her mind—of the Slipper Killer now began to get out of control.

"What is he like?" she said involuntarily.

Mr Bridie looked at her in mild inquiry, holding the car door. Jeremy quietly locked up and slipped into the back seat.

"I—I mean the Slipper Killer. Nash. You must remember him, don't you? It wasn't so very long ago."

Mr Bridie absently started the engine and manoeuvered the old car out the gate before answering. Then he said, "Nash was just a poor young fellow. Little harm in him. He knew a deal about birds and wild flowers—probably more than anyone else in these parts."

"Who was he? Do his family live in the village? Do we know them?"

"Nash is of no importance, I assure you," Mr Bridie said earnestly. "I understand, Miss Lindsay. You are worrying about the possibility of his having met little Carreen. But even if he had, she would be in no danger from him—unless he happened to find her picking a rare orchid, hardly a probability at this time of year." His smile was indulgent. "No, you can dismiss Nash from your mind, I promise you. If only the police would do so too! But of course it is their duty to find him. Really, it would be better, as I keep telling—" He bit off his sentence in order to negotiate one of the hairpins of the zigzag track. The visibility was very bad. By now the incessant crazy fluttering of the snow was beginning to tire their eyes, and Mr Bridie's ancient windscreen wiper could hardly keep pace with it. Deborah knew that the breakneck drop must be only a couple of feet away to the side of them, but she was too miserable to be nervous.

"You were saying—" she prompted him.

"Was I? I forget. Really, you know, I am sure you will find the little girl with Mrs Morne. Very likely she wrote a note for you and then forgot to leave it."

But Carreen was not at the Trout, and the shocked whiteness of Mrs Morne's face, the tensity of Willie, back from another ski-run, seemed to shake Mr Bridie for the first time into full awareness of the situation's possible gravity.

Mrs Whitelaw came into the parlour and exclaimed in horror; Jeremy moved brusquely past the chattering group and made for the telephone. Deborah quietly disentangled herself and slipped across the green to Mrs Lewthwaite's house. But there was no answer to her knock and she found the door locked when she tried it. She returned to the Trout. Several local people had by now come into the parlour and, having learned that a little girl was missing, were adding their suggestions to the general clamour.

Mrs Morne was exclaiming in a high-pitched voice, "But she *must* be *somewhere*. She can't just have *vanished*. Do you suppose the doctor called before you got back and took her off with him?"

"There wouldn't have been time." Jeremy was tight-lipped and grim. "He must be still on his way to hospital."

"But it's too *terrifying*—my poor little Carreen! In all this snow! What about Mrs Lewthwaite? What does she say?"

"She's not at her home," Deborah put in quietly. "We don't know where she is either."

Mrs Morne whisked round on Deborah with a sort of elegant ferocity. "Well, my dear, I hate to say I told you so, but I did *mention,* didn't I, that Mrs Lewthwaite was rather an odd person to leave in charge of the child?"

"You didn't give a reason," said Deborah, trying to keep the impatience out of her voice. "She was Mr Gilmartin's housekeeper—surely that's a guarantee of respectability? And what else could I do? She was the only person in the house. What's the matter with Mrs Lewthwaite?"

"Why," said Mrs Morne flatly, "only that she's the mother of Jock Nash, this precious Slipper Killer. Naturally she's bound to be a bit—shall we say, preoccupied at the moment."

A shocked gasp went round the room—but it was not a gasp of surprise. Deborah, looking quickly round, came to the conclusion that she and Jeremy were the only two people to whom the announcement came as news. The others in the parlour were simply horrified at a disgraceful fact being publicly proclaimed. It was affront at the mention of the black sheep in a gathering where strangers were present.

But Jeremy's surprise was genuine, Deborah was ready to swear. And she could see that he was thinking, putting facts together in rapid sequence, as she was herself. This added up, and this, and this—Mrs Lewthwaite's oddness and distress, the face at the window that first night—presumably Nash looking for his mother in the house where he knew she worked? And the broken wall, the traces of an intruder in the pigsty—had the pigs been turned out for a night while Nash sheltered in their straw—she would not dare put him in her own house—and was that why they had caught cold? Had Nash slipped into Herondale House and taken the pistol while they were all out looking at the pump?

Deborah's mind took her further. The open window and soaked bed in John Gilmartin's room—could Nash have been responsible for that? Or the slashed pump-rope? Or the assault—if assault it had been—on Carreen in the bathroom? Or the brakes of Jeremy's car? These hardly seemed like the actions of the personality Mr Bridie's remarks had built Nash into: a harmless, simple creature who had killed once to avenge the despoliation of a precious flower.

Was it Nash she ought to fear—or some keener intelligence using the identity of Nash as a cloak to cover its own vicious purpose?

"You told the police?" Mrs Morne was cross-examining Jeremy. "What did they say?"

"I talked to Leigh police station. They're in touch, by walkie-talkie, with the lot out searching for Nash. They've been alerted to look for Carreen too."

"But in the meantime," said Willie Rienz briskly, "there is nothing to stop us going out to look for the child. Who will volunteer to help?"

Several voices answered him.

"But is it safe?" Mrs Morne let her words trickle coldly into the following pause. "It looks as if Carrie must be with Mrs Lewthwaite, and obviously *she* will be with her son, or on her way to warn him that the police are looking for him —so anybody looking for Carrie is likely to find Nash."

"But he's harmless enough, Marion," Mr Bridie said irritably. "Everybody here knows that."

Mrs Morne shot him a glance of veiled animosity.

"After five years in prison? How do we know what he has turned into?"

"He has got a gun." Deborah spoke with diffidence; nevertheless all the heads turned in her direction as if pulled by strings. "At least he may have," she added, and explained how the pistol came to be missing.

"And you never told anyone?" Mrs Morne said accusingly. Deborah couldn't withstand the feeling that Mrs Morne was extracting a peculiar satisfaction—almost triumph— from the awfulness of the situation.

"I told Jeremy," she answered calmly.

"And I told the police," Jeremy said with equal calm.

"Well, that puts rather a different complexion on matters," Willie Rienz exclaimed. "We can hardly ask our good friends and neighbours to face an armed killer—" Deborah heard Mr Bridie murmur in gently acidulated tones, "Nash is *not* a killer"—"in order to look for our runaway niece. But I of course shall go and I expect our young friends here will come with me." He looked suggestively at Jeremy and Deborah, who nodded.

"Naturally they will!" Mrs Morne's high voice cut in. "After all they were responsible for this situation! If they hadn't gone off, leaving the child all alone in charge of a murderer's mother—"

"Oh, really, Marion!" Mr Bridie snapped with extreme dislike. "You know Susan Lewthwaite as well as I do. When you had a house in Herondale she used to work for you— you'd nothing against her then—"

The letters, Deborah thought. It was Mrs Lewthwaite's handwriting on the letter from Herondale House in Mrs Morne's suite at the Arundel Hotel. She was Mrs Morne's correspondent in Herondale. Susan Lewthwaite. Where had the name Susan come up recently? It seemed a solid, sober, domestic name, but somebody had gasped it out as if in fear and astonishment—who could it have been?

Cudgelling her wits, she remembered presently that the highly-strung Mrs Bligh had called out to some unseen Susan as she fainted. She had come out with the quilt, looked at Jeremy, flung up her hands, and gone down as if she had been pole-axed. But why had she called out something about Susan? The daughter's name was Rose; Rose was the only one at home. Mrs Bligh had a faintly familiar look, though; could there be a family connection?

Deborah edged through the crowd to Mrs Whitelaw. "Can you tell me," she said quietly, "is Mrs Bligh, at the farm up the valley, any relation to Mrs Lewthwaite?"

Mrs Whitelaw threw her a scared, distracted glance. "Well," she began doubtfully, "I promised I'd not gossip a word about yon family, but I can't see what harm there is in telling that: aye, Maggie Bligh is own sister to Susan Lewthwaite."

Deborah had a sensation of triumph, as if a key had turned in a lock.

"Would there be any chance that Mrs Lewthwaite had gone up to her sister's?"

"Nay, luv, it's very unlikely. They was at daggers drawn. Maggie would have nowt to do with Susan after the—after the trouble. In fact she disapproved of Susan's life altogether. And naturally that upset Susan very much—well, you do expect your own kinfolk to stand by you in bad times, don't you? No, she'd not have gone up to Blighs'."

Mrs Whitelaw moved away to superintend the bar, which was doing a brisk trade, and left Deborah to her mental gymnastics.

Mrs Bligh was Mrs Lewthwaite's sister, therefore aunt of Nash, the murderer. However much she had dissociated herself from her sister's troubles, she must still be nervous and concerned at the thought that her nephew was wandering loose in the vicinity. Everybody in the village was worried about him. Had Mrs Bligh ever been fond of her nephew? Or was she merely scared to death of him? What was there in the appearance of Mr Bridie, Deborah, and Jeremy, to make her faint dead away?

Deborah came out of her thoughts to hear Jeremy's impatient voice: "Well, if we're going, let's go," he was saying. "Have you got chains on your car, Rienz?"

"I had them fitted this morning. And I have a large-scale map. You are familiar with this district, are you not?"

"I've spent some holidays here," Jeremy said coolly. "I can pilot you about. Are you coming, Aunt Marion?"

"Good heavens, no! Someone has to be here in case the poor child turns up. Besides, I can feel one of my migraines coming on. All this is *very* distressing to me."

"Supposing the poor child turns up at Herondale House?" Jeremy pointed out.

"I will take a trip up there from time to time," Mr Bridie offered. "I fear that with my wretched malarial tendency I should only be a liability for any prolonged search over the fells . . ."

He let his sentence tail off and everyone thought unhappily of the miles and miles of snow-covered heather and shale, rock and scree and cliff and gully, treacherous with bogs and pot-holes, where the most experienced walker could be lost for days together in bad weather.

Willie Rienz was buckling himself into an elaborate leather coat and cap. Deborah pulled on a pair of gumboots borrowed from the inn. Jeremy was quietly imparting to Mr Bridie some last-minute suggestion for intercepting the doctor in case he was seen going up to Herondale House.

Good-natured, cheerful Mrs Whitelaw suddenly burst into tears. "Oh, I do hope you find the poor little lass," she sobbed. "If there's one thing I can't abide, it's a child lost."

A child lost . . . Jeremy, holding the door of the Daimler for Deborah, wondered what echo these words called up in his mind, and then remembered Carreen's conversation on the drive up from Leigh. "Small doll lost, wearing Blue Dress. Apply With In."

"Don't look so stricken. She's sure to turn up," he said to encourage Deborah, white and miserable in the back seat, and then he took his place by Willie in front and pulled out the map.

"I suggest we search the moor about Herondale House first of all," Willie said, "as that is nearest to the house it seems to be the obvious choice for a start. And the police have not yet been up there, I think."

"Okay," said Jeremy. "You take the track up to the House but keep left at the fork just before the gate."

"I am in your hands," Willie remarked, and let in the clutch.

They seemed to have been driving for hours. Every half-mile or so, Willie stopped the car and they all piled out and took different lines across the moor, searching and calling, investigating all darker objects in the prevailing grey of snow and mist. Inevitably these turned out to be rocks, or clumps of whin, or startled sheep who staggered to their feet and galloped away.

Deborah was beginning to feel desperately tired. They had had no lunch, and it must by now be hours past the time. Her hands were frozen, in soaked woollen mittens, and the snow had come over the tops of the borrowed gumboots and shaken into a layer of ice packed round her ankles.

After what seemed about the twentieth stop, as they were climbing back into the car, she suggested,

"Wasn't there a cave down the valley that was connected with Nash in some way? Was it that the Lady's-Slipper Orchid grew nearby? Would there be any point in searching there, do you suppose?"

"At Blind Man's Crag, you mean?" Jeremy said. "I was wondering about that. Nash took me there once when we were boys. It's odd, you know, I never associated him with the Slipper Killer—we used to call him Jock and I always assumed his surname was Lewthwaite. I suppose his mother married twice. He was a queer, dreamy boy—some of the boys used to call him Loopy Lewthwaite, but he wasn't mad, really, just simple, a bit visionary; I suppose what you'd call retarded. I rather liked him. I think I could find the cave again—there's a gully, where a stream runs down to the river."

"That is an intelligent suggestion," Willie agreed. "Let us go on in this direction for another mile or so and then turn back. After all a cave is a more probable hiding-place than the open moor."

Hiding-place for what? Who are we really looking for? Deborah wondered wearily. They passed a little stone moorland bridge, a clump of rowans, dark amid the flying snow, and paused to look under the bridge.

"There is a flask of hot coffee in the back, Miss Lindsay," Willie said when they re-entered the car. "Have some, and pass it to Mr Gilmartin."

The coffee was strong and welcome, even if it did have the tinny, metallic flavour of all drinks kept hot in vacuum flasks. At least it was hot. Deborah passed it to Jeremy, who offered it to Willie. He shook his head.

"Thank you, no. You two share it. I will take one of my pills." He opened a little compartmented silver snuff-box full of pills, red and black. "The red for pep-up, the black to tranquillise," Willie said, smiling, taking two red pills. "So! And what does your study of the map suggest now, Mr Gilmartin?"

"This track forks in about another mile," Jeremy said, folding the map and recorking the flask. "If we take the left fork we presently reach what looks like a barn. I suggest we take a look at that and then turn back. We must have come about ten miles and it's really ridiculous to assume that Carreen could have come half as far."

"Unless she was transported in some vehicle against her will?"

"We don't know that Nash could even drive," Jeremy pointed out. "And where would he have got a car?"

Willie shrugged.

Deborah began to be lulled by the hypnotic flicker of the snow on the windscreen, and the lurching sway of the car as Willie skilfully guided it on and on along the narrow track.

"Here's the barn," he said presently. It loomed ahead, a broken-down shape among the swirling shadows.

"Do you know," said Deborah, dragging herself from depths of drowsiness, "no one suggested we ought to bring a gun. But if Nash is in there——"

"I don't believe in guns," said Jeremy shortly. "Nasty, melodramatic things. People wave them about, they go off, and then someone's dead—generally some harmless person who'd just gone out to post a letter. I'd sooner trust to my wits."

"Very praiseworthy sentiments." Was there a trace of mockery in Willie's voice? Deborah was too sleepy to decide. "But I do not entirely agree with you. I went so far as to bring a gun, following your English precept, 'Better safe than sorry.' We can therefore investigate the barn with confidence. I will lead the way."

He got out of the car, turning to say, "If Miss Lindsay feels uneasy, perhaps she would prefer to remain?"

"No, I'll come," said Deborah, annoyed. "I'm so sleepy, perhaps the cold will wake me up a bit."

Jeremy helped her scramble out, turned to pick up one of his gloves which had fallen to the floor of the car, and then strode ahead of her after Willie.

The cold air did nothing to clear Deborah's head. She wondered, confusedly, if she had suddenly been overtaken by Carreen's flu. As she stumbled after Jeremy her eyes kept closing in spite of themselves. She came up violently against the cold granite of the barn wall and leaned against it in a spasm of weakness while the figures of the men disappeared round the corner.

". . . WILD GOOSE CHASE," boomed the voice of Rienz suddenly in her ear. "No roof on it."

"The barn's just a ruin, drifted up with snow." Jeremy was

beside her. "We might as well turn back. Deborah! Are you all right?"

"I feel—rather queer." Deborah swayed as she took a step.

"Here, hold up, girl! We'll get you back to the car." Jeremy's voice was full of concern.

"I regret—that is not possible."

Deborah stared disbelievingly, wondering if she was having hallucinations. Willie, who had already slid into the driver's seat, was pointing a gun at them through the car window. "I grieve to leave you thus, my young friends, but the drug you have swallowed will make your sufferings from the cold of mercifully short duration. Soon you will be in a deep, deep sleep, only to wake in Paradise."

"The—the coffee—" Deborah managed to articulate.

"Nothing harmful, my dear Miss Lindsay. Just a little sedative to encourage you to lie down in the snow and go to sleep. They say death from exposure is painless, even pleasant, do they not? Just a peaceful drowsiness, turning soon to the final coma. *Your* end may be a little slower, Mr Gilmartin—perhaps your resistance to drugs is greater—"

The squat little gun glinted in the last grey daylight. That's not John Gilmartin's gun, Deborah thought, with a faint spurt of mental activity; his was bigger, there must be another gun somewhere.

"I go now to find Carreen," Willie went on. "It was a good suggestion of yours, Miss Lindsay—that she might be in the cave at Blind Man's Crag with Mrs Lewthwaite, who will undoubtedly have gone to warn her son of the police search. I had intended to go there as soon as I had disposed of you and Mr Gilmartin."

"How will you find it?" snapped Jeremy.

"Marion knows its whereabouts."

"Marion?" I must follow what he is saying, Deborah thought, I must keep awake.

"She, too, went there when she was a child. Without doubt we shall find the little Carreen there. Alas that she will have been done to death by this escaped maniac."

"Supposing she's not there?" said Jeremy through stiff lips.

"If not—why then she will be somewhere else. Life is long —but somehow I cannot believe that the life of this gifted child will be so very long. Alas! The young Mozart, the young Shelley, now this poor young Carreen Gilmartin . . ."

"Haven't you forgotten something?" said Jeremy. "The ignition key . . ."

"I noticed you drop your glove, prudent Mr Gilmartin. But I regret your forethought was in vain, your little ruse has come to nought. I always carry a spare key."

With an oath, Jeremy flung himself forward, ignoring the threat of the gun. But the Daimler engine purred to life, the wheels spun and twisted in the snow, and, like a great ghost, the car vanished into a wilderness of whirling flakes.

"Damn . . ." said Jeremy. He tossed the ignition key away and it sank out of sight. "I should have realised from the start that he was the brains of that combination. It's hard to believe people are as twisted as you know they must be. Deborah! DEBORAH! Wake up!"

"I know," murmured Deborah through tissued layers of sleep. "But, Jeremy, I can't. What's the use? You'll be asleep too, very soon . . ."

"No I shan't." He shook her vigorously, went on shaking her. "I wasn't such a charley as to drink that bootlaced coffee; luckily the Daimler had a nice thick carpet. I just sprinkled it on the floor. I've had my doubts about Willie all the time. I shan't go to sleep—or not from the coffee, anyway. But we've got the devil of a way to walk, and no chance of a lift up here, I fear. Come on." He tugged her along. "That's the way, my dear. One foot after another. You'll walk it off after a bit—I hope to god," he added internally.

"But Carreen—he's sure to get to her first." Despair, even more incapacitating than the drug, held up Deborah's progress.

"There's always a hope that he may be wrong. She may not be there. We've got to bank on it. And once we're back he's sunk—you see that, don't you? Now he's admitted his intentions to both of us we have only to tell the police and he'll never dare lift a finger against Carreen again. Come on, ducky! Keep walking."

JOAN AIKEN

Deborah's head felt as large and formless as a cloud of smoke, but somehow she contrived to pick up first one foot and then the other, planting them in a carefully straight line through the snow. Jeremy's firm grasp guided her forward.

"It was Willie?" she said. "All the time? I thought it was you."

"You were meant to think so. And I thought it was you. Well, no," said Jeremy. "I didn't quite think that, but I did think you were in Marion's pay to bear false witness against me when it came to the point and to—to help her ends where possible. It wasn't till today when I saw how upset you were about Carreen that I was sure I was mistaken and that you really didn't know what they were planning. And when Willie doped you . . ."

"It was Willie all along," she said again. "You suspected him from the start?"

"I know my aunt Marion's capabilities," he said wearily. "Particularly when she has an able and unscrupulous partner. As Carreen was refusing to be their golden goose any longer, they had obviously decided it was time to cut their losses in regard to her and aim for the Gilmartin money. Are you listening?"

"Yes," Deborah said muzzily.

"Well pay attention. It's good for you to concentrate." He shook her again and quickened the pace. "Willie must have nipped up and cut the pump-rope and tampered with my brakes the day before yesterday when he brought up Carreen's luggage."

"Not the brakes," Deborah pointed out with hazy justice. "He couldn't have fixed those then. He must have done that later, at night. But he could have located the bathroom window, so he could come back later and attack Carreen. She was nearly drowned."

"That was what he did, was it?" Jeremy said. "I thought as much. What happened—you heard a noise and went in?"

"I didn't see him—I found her out cold in the bath with a bump on her head—gave her artificial respiration . . ."

"Good girl," said Jeremy warmly. "Come on, now! Faster! We've *got* to get back."

"But what about Nash? Where does he come in to this?

And Mrs Lewthwaite? And who—and what caused your uncle's death?"

"Nash is only incidental—in a way." Jeremy paused. "I think Willie and my aunt have been—with great adroitness —using the fact of his presence in the neighborhood as a cover for their own activities. They wanted both Carreen and me out of the way, so Nash was a godsend to them. If anything happened to Carreen, suspicion could point either to me, trying to double my legacy, or to Nash. It was to their advantage that Nash should remain at large as long as possible—that's why they've had to quicken the pace of their attempts at murder now the police have got here."

"And if *you* are found dead—"

"Nash again. Or, even neater—you and I both died gallantly from exposure, searching for Carreen."

"And your uncle—what happened to him?"

"Uncle John—poor old boy. There, I think Willie and Marion weren't responsible. I daresay I'll get it out of Dr Rumbold in the end but he's naturally cagey. Going between the lines of what I got out of the hospital, I think what happened was something like this: Nash got back to the village, found his mother's cottage shut, went up to Herondale House, where he knew she worked, couldn't make her hear—Mrs Lewthwaite is a bit deaf, remember— climbed up the creeper and in at my uncle's window. Being a bit simple, what they call a 'natural,' I suppose it didn't occur to him to shut the window, he just clambered in and left it wide. Went downstairs, found his mother—joyful reunion, tears, fright, decision to hide him in the pigsty, probably a lot of time wasted in giving him a meal and fixing him up with bedding out there—and when she remembered to go up and look at poor old Uncle John the rain had been beating in on him for a couple of hours. She was terrified and conscience-stricken—moved him to another room and bed, gave him hot compresses and so forth, but by that time pneumonia had set in."

"Poor woman," said Deborah, appalled. "So Nash killed him! Do you suppose the doctor knew that?"

"I'll bet he suspected it. But the hospital told me that death would have been only a matter of days in any case.

And in the circumstances I suppose the doctor wasn't going to add to the wretched Mrs Lewthwaite's distress over her son by bringing up the fact over the death certificate."

"You think he realised it was Nash?"

"I gathered from Bridie just now that everyone in the village guesses Nash is somewhere about. Everyone knows it's only a matter of time before the police find him. But they're a clannish lot. Wild horses wouldn't make them give anything away. Just about everyone's fond of Mrs Lewthwaite."

"But the sister—what about her?"

"What sister?"

"Mrs Lewthwaite's sister—Mrs Bligh, at the farm where we met the doctor. She hasn't had anything to do with Mrs Lewthwaite since the Slipper murder, apparently. Why did she faint when she saw you? I was thinking—I'd begun to think that you—"

"That I was the Slipper Killer and she fainted because she recognised me?"

"The doctor looked at you very oddly too."

"Probably the sight of me gave him a turn, reminded him of Uncle John."

"Do you think that can have been it?"

"I can only repeat," Jeremy said drily, "that I am not the Slipper Killer, though you seem unflatteringly ready to believe that I must be."

"Only because of the queer way Mrs Bligh behaved."

"I daresay she had a bad conscience because she'd been mean to her sister, and was ready to faint at the sight of any strange young man. Nash must have been in everyone's minds, plainly, though they wouldn't say anything to an outsider."

"That's why everyone closed up when he was mentioned . . . Why did Mrs Lewthwaite write letters to your aunt?"

"Did she? I don't know. Probably Aunt Marion paid her to keep her posted about Uncle John's state of health. Or had some hold over her. Aunt Marion's good at making people do things."

"Yes." It's a family trait, Deborah thought. Who else but Jeremy could have made me plod all this way through the snow, when my feet feel like thousand-pound weights, and my head is just an empty bubble floating through the air?

"What did she do to you, ducky?" Jeremy surprised her by asking. "I noticed her putting the screws on you at the funeral tea—she seemed to have got you fairly panicked. What was all that about? Come on—confession is good for the soul."

"Well—it was a small thing, really, I suppose, but *horrible*. I can't be sure that she actually engineered it—"

To her own surprise, Deborah found herself telling Jeremy all about the episode of the necklace.

"Ah yes," he said. "Jade and silver, I remember. No wonder you looked so glum when Aunt M. produced it." He was acutely interested in the story, made her go into every detail, questioned her minutely on each point.

"First you wrote an answer to the ad.; then you filled in a form; then you had a screening interview—all this before you actually saw Aunt Marion?"

"Yes."

"And you don't even know if she saw any other applicants besides you?"

"No."

"It would have been a pushover to rig the business at the shop, and pin it on you, to make sure you were thoroughly cowed and compliant. She goes through all the applications, picks out a suitable patsy—and you seem a perfect one if you don't mind my saying so, sweetheart, a nice, simple, innocent, straightforward, friendless Orphan Annie ready to be moulded to her requirements. She should have noticed that obstinate chin and that unnerving grey stare, though."

"Oh," said Deborah, "now I see something. It had been puzzling me: just before I came to Yorkshire my landlady told me that a man had been there asking all about me. She said he was 'not tall, but quite the gentleman'—that could have been the man who said he was the store manager. I suppose he was checking up on my story, and when they found I'd had all my things stolen and all my articles refused, I must have seemed a good choice. But even so—" With difficulty she swallowed a yawn, "even if she did pick me as the ideal sucker, I don't see quite how she could fix the necklace business. She couldn't be sure I'd pick anything up and put it down. She couldn't *hypnotise* me."

"She didn't have to. She sent you off to Port and Bellingham's with a long list of stuff to buy in the Christmas rush. In those crowds, waiting about to be served, you were almost bound to pick something up, handle some article, in a way that could afterwards be twisted to look compromising."

"But how did she manage about the witnesses? She couldn't have the whole staff in her pocket. I saw the salesgirl myself, selling stuff at the counter, she was genuine all right."

"My guess is," said Jeremy, "that the two chaps were both hired by Aunt Marion. Shady little private eyes, probably, that sort of character. One or both would follow you about the store, watching for a suitable opportunity. When it came they'd plant something on you that could afterwards be 'discovered.' And then tell the salesgirl, and come along for a showdown scene with Aunt Marion."

"Supposing I'd discovered the necklace in my pocket before that, and returned it—or hidden it?"

"They'd do something else some other time. In any case there would still be the smear and the suspicion—three accusing witnesses, even if nothing was proved."

"But how could they get the girl to give evidence?"

"By bribery or coercion of some kind—or they may have persuaded her that she really thought she'd seen you take it. She seemed tired and overworked, you say, and probably scared of losing her job. She must have believed they were bona fide store detectives—they may even have *been* bona fide store detectives and that's what gave Marion the idea in the first place. Stores hire a lot of odd extra birds when the rush begins."

"You seem to know a lot about it," Deborah said sleepily.

"I've been around in my time—worked in stores when there wasn't a freighter going my way."

"But," said Deborah, "all this—all this plot seems so complicated and devious—just to put me in an awkward spot. Doesn't it?"

"Not if you know Aunt Marion. And if you think of all

the cash at stake. She wanted to stay in England to keep an eye on Uncle John's last days and testamentary dispositions. She had to comply with educational regulations by having a qualified person to teach Carreen."

"Oh," Deborah suddenly burst out miserably, "Jeremy, *where* do you suppose Carreen is? I'm just worried to *death* over her. I can't bear to think about what might be happening . . ."

"Don't think about it, ducky. It doesn't do a bit of good. We're doing all we can . . . Come on, tell me some more about Aunt Marion. I'm trying to distract you, don't you see?"

"Well," Deborah said disjointedly, "one of the two men who gave evidence against me—there was a picture of him on Mr Bridie's desk."

"Mr *Bridie's* desk? When did you see this? What sort of picture?"

"This morning—when we were drinking sherry and waiting at his house. It was a newspaper cutting, and there was a caption, something about a court case—I can't remember exactly—"

"Queer," said Jeremy. There was a frown in his voice. "I can't think what the connection is there. I don't know what to make of Bridie—he's an odd fish."

"You don't think he could be the Slipper Killer? He keeps orchids . . ." Deborah stooped to scoop a rim of ice out of her boot with numb fingers; she swayed as soon as she stopped moving, and Jeremy grabbed her arm. "He gives me the shivers, rather."

"He's too old," Jeremy said, urging her on again. "Besides, he's been living in the village all the time. Maybe he's related, though—do you suppose he could be Nash's father?"

"Mr Bridie and Mrs Lewthwaite?" Deborah tried to consider this juxtaposition, but failed; they remained an obstinately incongruous couple. "It seems so unlikely . . ." The ground sideslipped and whirled up at her. Jeremy caught her arm again. "I'm sorry," she muttered, "I don't *mean* to keep doing this."

"It's lucky Willie didn't make the dose any stronger."

"Willie was trying to persuade me this morning—"

"Oh? Persuade you to what?"

"I don't quite know," she said drowsily. "Co-op—to co-operate over Carreen. Make her start writing again. I said no."

"There you are—you see where obstinacy lands you. If you'd said yes I suppose you'd be warm and dry at this moment."

"He was—queer." With a sleep-dulled mind and heavy tongue Deborah sought for some means of expressing Willie's aura of charged, dynamic potency in the brief conversation they had had; failing to find words she gave up. "He said another thing—"

"Keep moving, ducky."

"He said Marion's husband had left her. I'd thought she was a widow."

"So'd I. Don't blame him for walking out."

"It was because—because she was unstable. There was something else, too—something rather frightening—"

What had it been? Something related to Jeremy himself. But her drugged mind would not make the effort to dredge for the memory.

She looked up dazedly and saw the long streamers of snow speeding towards her out of the grey-blue dusk, endless white ribbons nearing and passing, to pile up soundlessly on the track; already the snow was up to their knees . . .

"I'll never make it, Jeremy," she whispered. "I'm just too tired. You mustn't bother about me. I'll stay here quietly; you go on—you can get back to the village on your own. Walk fast—get back—do something about Carreen—"

"Don't talk rubbish, ducky," said Jeremy kindly. "Who d'you think you are—Oates? You're going to get back if I have to drag you. So don't be lazy."

He put an arm round her shoulders and urged her along. She moved weakly but obediently; her legs felt like boiled macaroni.

"It's nice of you to try and save my life," she said with drowsy lucidity, "considering the nasty thoughts I've been having about you for the last three days . . ."

"Have you, duck?" Jeremy tucked his hand, holding hers, into her parka pocket.

"I thought you were sinister. I thought you'd killed John Gilmartin . . ."

Her voice trailed off. "Why, bless your heart," said Jeremy good-naturedly, "I was at sea the night that window was opened on Uncle John, standing watch on the *Duchess of Holdernesse*. I found his letter at my bank when we docked at Hull that morning. So I bought the old car and started for Herondale straight away. I just missed him . . . Hey, girl! *Wake up!*"

But Deborah had crumpled against him, past waking. Resolutely he knelt in the snow, tied her hands together with her scarf, looped her arms round his neck, and, rising, hitched her on to his back.

By now it was nearly dark. He set off walking at a slow, dogged pace.

Intense warmth. Brilliant colours. Flowers with great curving, waxy petals, the shape of antlers, or dragons' teeth——

"He said we'd wake in Paradise," Deborah murmured.

"Here, drink this. Hot milky coffee," somebody said. A face—a familiar, unexpected face loomed up right beside her, a cup was held to her lips. She sipped and choked on the scalding drink, but it roused her. Her vision cleared and she realised she was looking through a glass door at orchids growing in pots—at a brown and pink orchid with thick, fleshy leaves.

"Lady's-Slipper," she said, struggling upright.

"Never mind about the Lady's-Slipper—just keep still a moment till we get your hands untied," said Mr Bridie. "These knots have set like cement."

"Where's Jeremy?"

"He'll be back soon." Mr Bridie considered the knots and picked up a sharp knife. "Jeremy's just gone," he said grimly, "on an errand."

For Deborah, then, time began to flicker past in a vague and uncharted manner. One moment, it seemed to her, Mr Bridie was there, the next he was gone. A woman—his housekeeper—urged Deborah to drink her coffee and plied her with more. Her hands and feet were rubbed, she was dressed in warm, dry clothes.

"Where's Mr Bridie gone?" Deborah inquired, beginning to wake up and feel clearer.

"Out for the doctor. Try to walk about, miss, he said you were to keep moving. He won't be long." The woman withdrew.

Doctor? For whom? She, Deborah, was quite all right now, a little hazy, tired, aching, but perfectly in command of herself. Could it be—had they found Carreen? And where was Jeremy?

All of a sudden the room seemed a prison, with its quietly ticking clock—half past six, the hands said—fragrant flowers, blazing fire. Move about, Mr Bridie said. She was stiff and weak, her legs would only carry her in jerks, but with care she could guide them through the door.

Standing in the hall she saw the housekeeper running upstairs with a folded pile of towels.

"Is the search still going on?" Deborah said. "Is Mr Gilmartin with them? Did he see—Mrs Morne, Mr Rienz?"

The woman hesitated. "Yes," she finally said. "They're still out. Mr Gilmartin went straight off with them, down to Blind Man's Crag. Sergeant Herdman was there. Now you go back by the fire, miss. I'll bring you some more coffee in a moment."

She disappeared with her bundle round the head of the stairs. Deborah waited till her steps had died away, then quietly slipped out of the house. No outdoor clothes—but anyway, they were all soaking wet. She was wearing someone else's skirt and a sweater that looked as if it belonged to Mr Bridie. But it was only ten steps to the Trout Inn next door.

The gully slashed up the face of the hill, through scrubby trees. In the summer it would be concealed by brambles and nettles but now, in the snow, in the light of ten torches, it was like a black scar against the white, with the water spreading wide, running inkily down over hard rock where the grass had been washed away. Already the edges of the stream were beginning to freeze, and up above, from the flat rock that lay like a lintel over the cave entrance, icicles dangled. Down below, the hidden river roared in its gully.

On the farther side, beyond the bridge, a fir plantation was just barely visible as a denser black against the snow.

"You'd best stay here, sir," Sergeant Herdman suggested, but Jeremy said, "No, I'm coming up."

The snow slipped and squeaked under their feet as they left the road and climbed diagonally. Soon the noise of the river drowned the sound of their progress; here it ran ten feet deep among spurs of rock through a series of pools and cascades.

"It was lucky for us you remembered this place," the Sergeant said. "The way Rienz had hidden his car in that plantation, we might have missed it."

"Of course we don't know Nash is here. Rienz may not have found him."

"It's a chance."

"It was a chance for me and Miss Lindsay that you came out along the moor road."

"Mr Bridie tipped us off," the Sergeant said. "Told us you'd gone off that way and he hadn't seen you come back. Ah, look at that now!"

White torchlight, flickering down on the snowy, tussocky slope, had picked out a crumpled chocolate wrapper, red and gold.

"Picnickers?" Jeremy suggested.

"Too new. No picnickers this time of year. And it's the kind Nash likes. Look at the dog."

The tracker dog was whining, eager at the leash. They reached the mouth of the cave and stood under the rock lintel, out of the snow, but no drier for the shelter because of the incessant splash and trickle of water from the roof. Their boots were ankle-deep in icy slush. But after a short distance the tunnel sloped uphill and lay firm on rock; here the cave divided and three passages ran off in different directions.

The dog seemed doubtful; whined, sniffed first at one passage, then another.

"Likely he's been wandering all about the cave," suggested a constable. "Or they're both in there and have gone different ways."

Sergeant Herdman was decisive. He sent men down all

three passages and posted himself at the division with Jeremy.

"If anyone tries to do a bolt for it, this is the way they'll come."

They stood waiting, listening to the loud, hollow tinkle of drips, and the crash and reverberation of the echoes as the men made their way along the passages.

Deborah walked straight into the Trout Inn, through the small glass-doored lobby and the hall with the stuffed fish and worn mats on the flagged floor. The public bar was open but the few customers in there were subdued and the talk that floated out through the door was low-voiced; there was no laughter. Mrs Whitelaw, her face drawn with anxiety, was serving behind the bar. When she saw Deborah she came out into the hall.

"No news yet of the searchers?" Deborah asked.

Mrs Whitelaw shook her head. "Nay, not yet." She looked at Deborah solicitously. "Are you all right, luv? You look terribly pale. Here, coom into the parlour and have a sit-down while I fetch you a drop o' summat—how about a hot toddy?"

"I won't, thanks," said Deborah, with a vague recollection that it was a mistake to mix drink and drugs. "I'm fine, really. Do you—is Mrs Morne about? I rather wanted to see her."

"She's oopstairs, having a bit of a lay-down—she came over queer with a migraine, and no wonder, with all this worry. I'll tiptoe oop and see if she's awake—she asked me to call her, anyway, if she wasn't down by seven. You sit there, luv—miss—and I'll see."

"Don't bother if she's likely to be down soon," Deborah said. "I'm sure you're busy."

"Make yourself comfortable, then, luv. I'll bring you a nice pot of tea in joost a minute. There's plenty of books if you want a nice read," Mrs Whitelaw added rather distractedly, and bustled back to her bar customers.

Tense and anxious as she was, Deborah couldn't help a wry grin as she surveyed the tattered piles of *Country Life* and *The Field;* even while waiting for possible news of a murder, evidently, the true Briton kept a stiff upper lip, as in the dentist's waiting-room, and leafed through the illustrated papers. She sat on the comfortable, baggy sofa, clutching the small strip of newsprint she had brought from Mr Bridie's, and waited. Five minutes passed and Mrs Whitelaw returned with a tray of tea-things.

"I can hear Mrs Morne stirring oopstairs," she said, and, going out into the hall, she called, "There's a pot of tea joost mashed, Mrs Morne," before returning to her bar duties.

Deborah absently poured herself a cup of tea, stirred it, and forgot to drink it. She wondered what sort of thoughts were passing through Mrs Morne's mind. How did it feel, waiting quietly in a snowbound country inn, while somebody was out in the blizzard murdering three people on your behalf?

Presently she heard feet coming down the stairs—a light, dragging tread—and next moment Marion Morne came into the room.

When Mrs Morne saw Deborah she jumped uncontrollably, as if her bones had started in their sockets. Her colour, already bad, became dreadful; she said something indistinguishable, reached out for the back of the nearest chair, and sat down on it heavily.

"I suppose you didn't expect to see me again?" Deborah said. "I'd been thinking that I must have dreamed or imagined what Willie told us, when he went off and left us, but now I can see that it was true. You meant us to die out there, Jeremy and me, didn't you?"

Mrs Morne had recovered a small vestige of her habitual composure. She poured herself a cup of tea, opened her handbag with deliberation, took out a phial, and shook into her hand a couple of pills, which she swallowed—but some of the tea had slopped into the saucer, and the cup shook and dripped as she raised it to her lips.

"My dear Miss Lindsay," she said. "I'm very worried and upset as you can imagine. I have a terrible headache. Will you kindly explain just what you are talking about. Has—is there any news yet of Carreen?"

A pulse twitched involuntarily in her cheek. She put up her hand to quiet it.

"No news yet," Deborah said. "You had better hope, though, that Jeremy and the police find Carreen before Mr Rienz does—otherwise you are going to be in bad trouble, Mrs Morne."

"Jeremy—police—what do you mean?"

"Your Babes-in-the-Wood plan failed," Deborah repeated carefully. "Jeremy didn't drink any of the drugged coffee. He stayed awake and brought me back, and now he's gone out with the police looking for Mr Rienz, and he's pretty hopping mad, I expect. Don't you think you had better tell me where Carreen is?"

"Drugged coffee? Are you crazy?" Mrs Morne pressed her fingers against her forehead as if she were trying to drive them right through the bone. "I think all this strain must be too much for you. I haven't the faintest idea what you're talking about."

Deborah said flatly, "You might as well abandon that line. Mr Rienz was quite explicit about your plans when he left Jeremy and me—as he thought—to die in the snow. Jeremy has probably given the police the whole story by now. So, will you *please* tell me, where is Carreen?"

Mrs Morne stood up. Her mouth open, soundlessly, she stared at Deborah as if, for the first time, the implication of what had been said struck home to her. She said, in a queer, harsh tone, unlike her usual voice, "How should I know? For heaven's sake don't keep bothering me, leave me alone, can't you? I tell you, I don't *know* where she is!" and moved with rapid, uncertain steps out into the hall. Deborah heard the ting of the pay-phone and, in a couple of minutes, the rattle of coins. Mrs Morne's voice came through the doorway.

"Leigh 214? Mr Brigg? Oh, this is Mrs Morne here, at Herondale. I wonder if you could come up to the Trout and collect me—I want to get the next train to Leeds. Yes, now. You—what? The snow? But, good heavens, you ought to be used to a bit of snow! *Listen*—I've *got* to get that train—it's urgent! Yes, urgent, I said. You mean you can't—well, isn't there anyone—oh, this is *ridiculous!*" The telephone quacked back at her emphatically and Deborah, who had moved quietly into the hall, recognised Mr Brigg's nasal tones.

"I never heard such nonsense!" Mrs Morne cried, her voice rising. "How can you be so disobliging? You're supposed to ply for public hire! Look, I'll give you double the fare—how about that? *Treble* the fare!" The telephone made a decisive noise and was silent; dazed, incredulous, Mrs Morne stared at the receiver in her hand.

"He rang off!" she said. "How dare he? He rang off!" Without looking at Deborah she turned and walked blunderingly back into the parlour.

The front door opened and two police came in, shaking off snow. Instantly the bar customers stopped their quiet chat and surged out to ask if there was any news. The men shook their heads. They were going up the beck, they said, and had merely called in for ropes to negotiate the cliff-face; the ones they had with them were not long enough, could Mrs Whitelaw help them? Mrs Whitelaw could, it seemed; the Trout always kept basic rescue equipment for weekend pot-holers who found themselves in difficulties. She offered the policemen hot drinks as well, but they refused and hurried out again, clumping and squeaking over the flags in their heavy boots.

Deborah turned to re-enter the parlour. By the door she stood stockstill, in the act of stepping over the threshold, galvanised by the sight, reflected in a mirror, of Mrs Morne quietly dropping half a dozen pills into her untouched cup of tea and giving it a quick stir. This done, she sat down again, and was drinking her own tea in short, nervous sips when Deborah walked back into the room. But she kept her eyes fixed on Deborah's cup and the pulse in her cheek fluttered again uncontrollably.

Deborah laid the newspaper cutting down before her.

"That is your husband, isn't it?" she said. "Thomas Franklyn Morne, jailed for two years on six charges of fraud, forgery, and embezzlement. When was that picture taken?"

"How dare you?" said Mrs Morne shrilly. "Where did you get that? How dare you?"

"From Mr Bridie's house. It was your husband who framed up the evidence against me, wasn't it?"

"Oh, be quiet!" Mrs Morne said. She tapped irritably on the table, and again pressed her knuckles against her forehead. "Be quiet and drink your tea and go away. Stop bothering me! I've got to make plans. Oh, heavens, how my head aches."

Mr Bridie came quickly into the room and stopped, when he saw them, with a look of relief. He, too, was powdered with snow.

"Plans?" he said. "I should not make too many plans at the moment, my dear Marion. They might have to be revised." He shook his head at Deborah, in reproof. "So that's where you got to, naughty girl! You gave us a fright, running out with no coat on like that!"

Mrs Morne stood up. She crossed to Mr Bridie with hasty steps.

"Richard! You have a car, haven't you? You don't mind a bit of snow, you'll drive me to Cranton, won't you? That miserable Brigg has let me down, and Willie's gone off god knows where, and I'm so *sick* of this damned place—I've got to get away. You'll do it for me, won't you—you know how I've always been f-fond of you, Rick!" Her words tumbled out in little spurts, she took hold of his lapels and looked up at him in a confiding manner that seemed ludicrously and pathetically incongruous.

Mr Bridie's eyes met those of Deborah. With fastidious care he disengaged himself from the shaking, clutching hands.

"Oh, my dear Marion," he said gently. "I'm afraid this touching appeal to my kind heart has come just about thirty years too late."

"This must be a pretty big cave, then?" the Sergeant said, stamping his feet on the rocky floor as they waited. "Will it go back a long way, do you know?"

"I never went in very far . . . I believe it's quite big. Not a pleasant place to have to hide." Jeremy shivered. As soon as he stopped walking he realised how tired he was. He felt once more as if he were making his hopeless way along the moor road, with Deborah's limp weight on his back and the snow cutting at his face. The deadly chill of the cave struck through his sodden clothes to the stiff and aching muscles in his back and arms. He shivered again at the very conception of bringing an ailing child to such a place as this.

"Ah!" said the Sergeant. "What was that?"

The sound of gunfire seemed to come from three directions at once as the echoes roared and fought in the cave's rocky vault. There were shouts, splashes, another shot. Jeremy and the Sergeant stood keyed-up, alert, but still undecided which way to move.

Suddenly there came the thunder of running feet and one of the constables appeared.

"He's shot him, sir!" he gasped.

"Who's shot who, you gowk?"

"Why, *he's* shot *him*—Nash. You'd best come quick, sir."

The constable hadn't waited. He had turned and was slipping and stumbling along the passage with Jeremy close behind. They ran what might have been a hundred yards, then the tunnel narrowed and lowered so that they had to stoop, and there was a sharp turn; beyond, it opened into a small grotto filled with wan flickering light from their torches and a couple of candles, high on a rock shelf.

The place was crudely furnished: a safari camp-bed with blankets, a couple of orange-boxes with some food on them; on the bed Jeremy noticed—and his heart was wrung with a curious feeling of kinship and pity—two leather-bound books that came, surely, from John Gilmartin's library: Hapgood's *British Wildflowers,* 1861, in two volumes, with coloured engravings.

Willie Rienz stood, indignant, between two constables. Behind him Jeremy could see the feet of someone lying on the floor.

"It was self-defense!" Willie said angrily. "The man would have killed me—he flew at me like a wild beast!"

"I heard him as I cam oop the passage, sir," a constable said. "Yon chap was saying to Nash, 'Wheer are they, then, wheer's Carreen and yer moother? Coom on, tell, and I'll gie ye a fiver; sitha, I'll not let on to t'police about you, man.' But Nash answers him niver a word, and then he flies at him, fair impatient, and shakes him like a collie dog, and shouts, 'Say wheer they are, ye stupid nowt!' and at that Nash gets his dander up and lets him have it, like, wi' his fists, and next thing this chap has his gun oot and shoots him reet i' the chest, point-blank."

"It was self-defence," Willie Rienz said again. "He had a gun. He would have shot me."

The Sergeant looked down at Nash's weapon, lying by the dead hand. "That old thing," he said pityingly. "Old John Gilmartin's pistol. That hadn't been fired since the Boer War. He'd never have shot you with that.—I must ask you to come down to the Station with me, to answer some questions about this business, sir."

"I see no reason for this! I was helping to apprehend an escaped criminal—and to look for my ward—"

"Oh, not only about Nash, sir. About Mr Gilmartin and Miss Lindsay."

"I know nothing of their whereabouts," Willie said glibly. "I left them at the gates of Herondale House when I went up to look for Carreen on the moor. They intended to search independently, on foot. No doubt they will turn up in due course. It is Carreen you should be worrying about, probably somewhere in this cave— Have you looked in the other passages, have you called?"

The Sergeant stepped aside and Willie suddenly saw Jeremy. A look of astonishment, almost incredulity, came over his face.

"How did you get here?" he ejaculated.

"You should have made quite sure I drank that coffee, Mr Rienz," Jeremy said.

Willie began a piece of furious self-justification. "You can prove nothing! I left you because you were holding up the search. In any case, I believe *you* killed your uncle—how do I know you have not killed Carreen too? If not, where is she?"

"If you'll come with us, we'll go into all that, sir," the Sergeant said.

Realising, but not accepting defeat, Willie suddenly flung aside the loose grasp of one of the constables, and made a bolt for the entrance.

"After him!" shouted Herdman angrily. They all ran, jostling each other. But Willie had a long start and, with his shorter stature, found it easier to dart through the long, narrow tunnel. He plunged out into the gusty dark. Streamers of snow carried the torchlight away from him as he ran careering and sliding down the slope.

"By god—" said the Sergeant. "If he gets to that car of his— Did anyone think to take the key?"

"It wasn't in the ignition, sir."

"Let the dog go, Holroyd!"

The dog bounded forward with a jerk, its extended body ribboning down over the rough ground, disappearing beyond an outcrop of rock, bobbing up again. Below lay the snow-swollen river in its hidden gully.

"This damned weather—"

Twisting his head, rubbing the snow out of his eyes, Jeremy floundered after the Sergeant, now feeling all his exhaustion. He could not keep up this pace much longer.

The men were strung out ahead.

"There he goes—! After him, boy!"

In a momentary gap between the white gusts they all saw the little figure of the man pause below them in a cleft of rock, hesitate, and then suddenly topple as the dog launched itself on him from above.

There was a faint, wailing cry; then the white spirals of snow blanketed the scene.

Mrs Morne had retreated into silence. She sat huddled, staring at the floor, her face averted from Mr Bridie and Deborah. Her lips were pressed together in a thin, petulant line. Ceaselessly she picked at the skin round her fingernails. She seemed on the verge of collapse; at every slight sound she started violently. Her face had somehow crumpled and sagged so that all its assertive elegance was gone —what remained was the sunk-in, cantankerous, self-absorption of an old woman.

Deborah felt a kind of uneasy pity for this wreck of her formidable employer and almost wished that she had been able to make her bolt in Mr Brigg's taxi. This business of waiting for exposure was horrible; it seemed to degrade them all. In books, Deborah thought, there is inevitably a lightning denouement and the villains are neatly whisked away. You don't have to sit with them like relatives waiting for the result of an operation. She wished now that she had not been spurred out of Mr Bridie's house by her anxiety over Carreen. And where was Carreen?

Noticing the newspaper cutting on the table, Mr Bridie put it back in his pocket, remarking drily,

"Ah, ye'd have done better to marry me, my dear Marion, poor as I was, than yon miserable fellow, Morne. Ye can see, I followed his downward career! What happened when he went to jail, you divorced him, got yourself clear out of that mess, eh? Aye, but tar sticks, doesn't it, and old habits die hard. Where is he now, I wonder? No wonder ye were anxious to rid yourself of him when you got your hooks on a young gold-mine like Carreen."

Mrs Morne twitched her head away impatiently but took no other notice of this speech. She seemed only half aware of their presence, now, as if she were trying to withdraw from reality entirely. Deborah, with a chilly foreboding, remembered Willie's remarks about the instability of the Gilmartin family.

"Do you think she's all right?" she murmured in a low, worried voice to Mr Bridie, "Are they really unbalanced—the Gilmartins, I mean?"

"Not that *I* ever heard. Who fed ye that load of moonshine?"

"Willie. He said they were all unstable—that Jeremy used to have mad rages when he was young. And some affair about a schoolmistress that had to be hushed up—"

Mr Bridie burst out laughing. "Aye, she fell in love with Jeremy's father and turned up in his bedroom. No, my dear gel, they're as sane as you or I—Willie was just trying to frighten you."

Mrs Morne started. Her ears, which had ignored their low-pitched talk, were the first to catch voices, steps, the crunch of tyres on the snow outside. The outer door rattled. Suddenly the place was full of policemen.

Deborah's eyes sought anxiously in the blur of dark-blue uniform until right at the back they found Jeremy, looking fine-drawn and deathly tired. His eyes met hers with a question in them which she was unable to answer.

Meanwhile several things were happening simultaneously.

"No, she wasn't there," Sergeant Herdman was saying to Mr Bridie. "But we found Nash—this man had shot him—"

For the first time Deborah noticed the limping figure of Willie, supported by a couple of burly constables in the middle of the group. His torn parka was soaking; there was blood on his forehead.

At the same moment, Marion Morne sprang forward with unbelievable venom in her expression.

"You miserable *fool!* I told you to leave matters alone! I told you there was too much risk!" She was so transported with rage that she pummelled Willie's chest with her fists, screaming at him like a madwoman.

"You told me!" he spat back at her. "I like that! Who put the pills in the coffee? Who had this clever notion of using the Slipper Killer—now see where you've landed us! And—just like a woman—you couldn't even put in enough pills!"

It was an extraordinary scene: like a grotesque parody of a matrimonial row. So absorbed were the participants in abusing each other that for a moment or two they did not notice the electric silence, in which their statements were received, or the shocked faces of the police. Then the men who were supporting Willie pulled him back, and Sergeant Herdman intervened.

"You'll have to explain what you're talking about, madam," he said to Mrs Morne. "What's this about pills?"

She seemed suddenly to recollect herself and, stepping back, sat down again at the table, resuming her previous cloak of blank, sullen disinterest. "It's nothing to do with me," she said. *"He* did it all. Everything. The car brakes, the pump-weight, knocking out Carreen in the bath—I wasn't even there, I can prove it!"

Willie started towards her, exclaiming furiously, but was brought up short by his two captors, and let out a sharp grunt of pain; Deborah saw there was something the matter with his leg.

"You put the pills in the coffee!" he repeated.

159

"They can't prove it. There are no fingerprints." Calmly she opened a compact, studied her face, and put on some powder.

"No, but they can prove you put the pills in my tea-cup!" Deborah suddenly exclaimed. Sergeant Herdman looked her way in surprise. "Mrs Morne did it when I was out of the room," she told him. "I saw her in the mirror—I suppose hoping, in some way, that she could get rid of me before the search-parties came back. I haven't touched it . . ."

"Put it in a bottle and bring it along, Holroyd," Sergeant Herdman said grimly, "We'd best take them down to the Station now, before we're snowed up."

"But what about Carreen?" cried Deborah and Jeremy simultaneously, and Deborah said, "What does it matter about them? You *can't* leave before you find her—!"

Mr Bridie stepped forward. He wore the most extraordinary expression: prim, complacent, smirking, like a barnyard fowl that has laid a peacock's egg.

"Ahem—I believe *I* can help on that point," he said delicately.

Mrs Morne turned on him a stare of fanatical dislike. Her eyes blazed.

"*You!* I might have guessed that you'd be at the bottom of it! You've always meant to get even with me, haven't you? Oh, why did I ever come back to this *loathsome, detestable* place? I can't *stand* it here!"

She glanced in a hunted way about the room—at the curious, hostile, watchful eyes that were all fixed on her; suddenly an idea appeared to strike her. Moving forward with her quick, blundering pace she picked up the full cup of tea and, before anyone could stop her, drank it off . . .

Deborah did not wait, in the hubbub that broke out then. The import of Mr Bridie's statement had come home to her. With a muttered word to Jeremy, she darted out of the inn parlour and ran through the snowy darkness to the house next door.

The firelight winked and flickered on Mr Bridie's prim brass fender. Mr Bridie's pale, pretty carpet was patched and stained with damp from the men's boots where they had stood, drinking the hot negus he had hospitably forced on them.

"Will she live, do you suppose?" Jeremy asked, into the silence.

"It's a toss-up, I'd say. Rumbold's working on her still. In any case, she'd be no loss. Eh, dear," said Mr Bridie unhappily. "Poor Nash! I'd rather *he* had lived. Rienz has got off lighter than he deserved with a broken leg."

"Still he has to stand his trial for manslaughter yet," Jeremy pointed out.

"It may not come to that, as Nash was an escaped criminal."

"Well, attempted murder, anyway."

"Maybe. Proudshaw's doubtful if there's enough actual evidence to convict, but that conversation in front of witnesses should help."

"Poor Mrs Lewthwaite," Jeremy said. "Has she taken it very hard?"

"In a way I think the worst was over for her days ago. She's finding comfort in looking after Carreen."

"I can't get over Carreen's having been here all the time," Jeremy said. "I ought to have guessed . . ."

Mr Bridie gave his demure, downy chuckle. "When you told me all that chapter of misfortune this morning, brakes and pump-weights and bathroom windows, I just thought to myself, Herondale House is no place for a little gel at present, so while ye were all around the village hunting for the doctor I popped up there in Rattletrap and brought Carreen and Mrs Lewthwaite back here. The quiet eye sees the most, so, thought I, I'll just wait a wee while and see which of them seems *really* anxious about Carreen before revealing my little deception. But indeed I might have known you were innocent enough in the matter. I might have guessed —soon, of course, I did guess—that it was Marion up to her tricks again. I knew she'd never let that money go without some double-dealing."

"Carreen and Mrs Lewthwaite have been here all day?"

"Snug and warm," said Mr Bridie with satisfaction. "Miss Deborah's with them now. It was time Susan Lewthwaite had a kindly roof over her head—the poor woman's been going half demented with worry and grief these last days. 'Susan,' said I, ye'd best tell the police that Jock's here,' and so thought many in the village. But she couldn't bring herself to do it—she was fair wearing herself out, hiding him first in one place, then another. 'He can't bear being shut up, Mr Bridie,' she says to me, tears in her eyes. But what was he, if not shut up, in barns and pigsties and caves?

"Maybe it's best as it is. Poor Nash. When he was in his right mind he'd not have harmed a fly. Well, you may remember him when he was a boy. He'd roam the woods and fells, he'd make up his bits of poetry and songs; he knew more about the wild things than any man in Yorkshire. The destruction of wild birds or wild flowers was the only thing that could get him in a rage, and then he didn't know his own strength. When he killed that wretched collector-fellow from Leeds who dug up the orchid, it was all over in a flash; then he carried the man five miles back to the village, crying like a baby. 'Oh, mother, see what I've done,' he says, 'but I had to do it. He was digging up my Lady's-Slipper.' "

Mr Bridie walked slowly through into his conservatory and stood there, gazing down at the face of the man who lay among the brilliant fragile flowers until the police could bring up the mortuary van next day.

"At least they won't shut him up again," he said. "He looks peaceful enough now, poor boy."

Jeremy joined him, and stared in bewildered astonishment. For the face of Nash Lewthwaite, innocent as that of a sleeping child, with dark hair tumbled back off his forehead, was an older version of the face of Carreen Gilmartin.

"Ah, I see ye didn't know," Mr Bridie said. "Aye, the family likeness is strong. He's very like you, too, my boy. He was old John's son. Nash was Susan Lewthwaite's maiden name. Many times John Gilmartin offered to marry her, but she was a proud woman. She wouldn't. There was mental trouble in *her* family, you see, and when she realised Nash had inherited it, she'd have no more to do with John—except to look after his house and see he got his meals."

"So that was why her sister fainted when she saw me."

"Aye, for a moment she'll have taken ye for Jock."

Mr Bridie fell silent, sighing; Jeremy stood motionless beside him. Both men were thinking of John Gilmartin's abrupt, unceremonious end, at the innocent hands of his own son.

"Aunt Marion knew, I suppose?" Jeremy remarked presently.

"Oh, aye, she knew."

"But why did Mrs Lewthwaite write to her?" Jeremy said, puzzled.

"Susan has a very strong sense of duty; when old John fell ill she thought Marion, as his nearest relative, ought to be kept informed of how he did. She cared for him faithfully— Lord knows he took little enough care of himself—but she's no fortune-hunter and didn't wish to be thought of as such."

"So," said Jeremy—and suddenly he chuckled wryly—"all this money Marion's been manoeuvring for oughtn't by rights to have come to us *or* to her. It should have gone to Nash and his mother. I'll tell Carreen. I know she'll want to make over—"

"Leave it, lad. Nash couldn't have inherited, poor simple soul, and his mother will not take a penny more than John left her. He had proposed to leave her the lot but she wouldn't have it—"

Deborah came downstairs. She gave Jeremy a shy smile.

"Carreen's had a long sleep and her temperature's right down. She's asking for you. The doctor's seen her and he says what she has is nothing but a feverish cold."

"Eh, but you're a stout-hearted young lady," Mr Bridie said admiringly. "Not much above three hours ago Jeremy brought you in looking like a frozen corpse, and here you are, lively as a cricket, running out into the snow again . . ."

"Mr Bridie," said Deborah. "What will happen to Mrs Morne? If she doesn't—if she recovers?"

"Eh, well," he rubbed his chin reflectively, "her lawyer may claim that she's unfit to plead. She certainly seemed fairly close to a breakdown. But in my opinion they'll not get away with it. I think they'll both get sentences."

"Prison, you mean? How horrible."

"Gracious goodness, you've no call to sympathise with her, my dear. She had you cast for the monkey's allowance whichever way things went. And she's been living on Carreen's money long enough, she and that precious husband of hers. I'd waste no sorrow on her."

"Husband? You mean Morne? Weren't they divorced?"

"Oh, aye, she divorced him quick enough. No, it turns out she was married to Willie; mainly a business partnership, I fancy, and they kept it dark, probably to dodge tax. It's all of a piece. Herdman's been through to the London police and got all the information about the Morne case: Morne was a fraudulent company promoter who got off with a lot of clients' money seven years ago, and there was little doubt that Marion was in it with him, but they hadn't enough evidence to bring it home to her."

"So she got a divorce and shook herself clear."

"That's about it. And then Carreen's parents died a couple of years later; Marion had picked up with Willie by then and he saw Carreen's potentialities—he's a very intelligent man, used to write plays himself that didn't take—so they just latched on to the child. It seemed a suitable enough arrangement, nobody objected. And all went well until Carreen began to grow up and find her feet."

"And till they picked Deborah for a governess," Jeremy said.

"Just so. Which coincided, unfortunately for them, with Marion overreaching herself in her greed to get hold of old John's money. It's ironic to think that he *had* intended to leave it to her, as Susan wouldn't touch it; if she'd treated Carreen a bit better, so that she hadn't sent off that appeal to her uncle which made him change his will, Marion and Willie would have been in clover by now. Ah well, they'll trouble you no more. You can dismiss them from your mind."

"Come along upstairs, then, Jeremy," Deborah said. "Carreen's dying to see you."

Jeremy gave her a dramatic scowl. "Don't bully me," he said, "or I shall pick you up and carry you. I've got your measure now, you featherweight! There's one good thing to be said for manhandling a girl three miles through the snow —it makes you a bit less nervous of her. When I think how you had me cowed, up at Herondale House, with all that icy politeness—"

"Oh, what rubbish," Deborah said, laughing. "It was you who had *me* cowed."

She ran ahead of him up the stairs.

Firelight danced on the walls and ceiling of Mr Bridie's neat little spare room with its chintz frills and floral wallpaper. Carreen, snug under a stiff pink satin quilt, bounced up ecstatically as Jeremy came in.

"Darling cousin Jeremy! Oh, I was so afraid you might have suffered some *mis*hap—!"

"Nothing ever happens to me, Picklepuss," he said, hugging her. "You ask Deborah here. It was you we were losing our hair over, my pretty little coz—we thought we'd lost you for sure!"

Mrs Lewthwaite came in with chicken broth and toast on a tray. She was pale and red-eyed but composed. "Here you are, love," she said, smiling kindly at Carreen. "Get that inside you before you try to chatter."

Deborah was startled and touched when Jeremy crossed to Mrs Lewthwaite and laid an arm round her shoulders. "We are all so sorry about your son," he said gently. "We do hope very much that you will come and live with us at Herondale House."

Mrs Lewthwaite went pink. Her eyes filled with tears again. "Eh, you're a good lad," she said gruffly. "I—I can see your uncle in you. I'll have to think about it—there's my little house he left me. But thank you kindly for the offer."

"Think about it hard," Jeremy said. "We want you to come."

"*Indeed* we do," echoed Carreen earnestly.

Mrs Lewthwaite gave them a tremulous smile, started to speak, failed, and hurried out of the room.

Deborah felt suddenly rather forlorn, outsider to this queer little family circle, so suddenly and warmly knit.

"Well," she said uncertainly, "I think if you'll excuse me—"

"Deborah, where are you going?" exclaimed Carreen. "Sit down here!" She thumped the pink quilt and added politely as an afterthought, "If you have no objection."

"She doesn't like us, I fear," said Jeremy mournfully. "It's going to be a terrible job to persuade this girl to stay in Herondale. She's going to hold things like that diesel fuel against me for the rest of my life."

"Deborah, *dear* Deborah," Carreen said, "you *will* stay with us and teach me arithmetic and spelling and the essentials of life, won't you? I suspect there are some fearful gaps in Cousin Jeremy's education, too, which you could fill in—plainly he has not been well brought up—and in return I am *confident* that he will be able to teach you the difference between petrol and diesel fuel."

"It's a fair offer," Jeremy said. "Well? Will you stay at Herondale?"

Herondale, Deborah thought. The wide, mysterious moors, the queer, secretive village. But now she understood that the secretiveness held no hostility in it. The village had been bound together out of loyalty to protect Mrs Lewthwaite's sad secret from the outside world. It would be a fine thing to belong in such a place, once the people had accepted you . . .

Deborah looked up at Jeremy. His eyes were dancing. "Tak' tha time considering, lass," he said. "No hasty decisions, now. But we can do wi' thee. Tha makes a gradely dish o' porridge, equal to any i' Yorkshire."

With a sudden access of confidence Deborah returned his mocking grin. He took her hand, pulling her to her feet.

"Coom oop, luv," he said, "I can hear Mr Bridie calling us down to supper."